W9-CUC-143

DIGGERS

DIGGERS

The Second Book
of the Bromeliad

TERRY PRATCHETT

**Delacorte
Press**

Published by
Delacorte Press
Bantam Doubleday Dell Publishing Group, Inc.
666 Fifth Avenue
New York, New York 10103

This work was originally published in Great
Britain by Transworld Publishers Ltd.

Library of Congress Cataloging in Publication Data

Pratchett, Terry.
    Diggers / Terry Pratchett.
        p.   cm.
    Summary: A group of small creatures called
nomes, whose families have lived for generations
hidden in a department store, are forced to flee to a
country quarry, where they struggle against harsh
weather, destructive humans, and dissension
among themselves.
    ISBN 0-385-30152-9
    [1. Fantasy.]   I. Title.
PZ7.P8865Di   1990
[Fic]—dc20   89-78123
                                                 CIP
                                                  AC

Manufactured in the United States of America

February 1991

10 9 8 7 6 5 4 3 2 1

BVG

In the beginning . . .

. . . Arnold Bros. (est. 1905) created the Store.

At least, that was the belief of thousands of nomes who for many generations* had lived under the floorboards of Arnold Bros. (est. 1905), an old and respected department store in the middle of the city.

The Store had become their world. A world with a roof and walls.

Wind and Rain were ancient legends. So were Day and Night. Now there were sprinkler systems and air conditioners, and the nomes' small, crowded lives ticked to the clock of Opening Time and Closing Time. The seasons of their year were January Sales, Spring into Spring Fashions, Summer Bargains, and Christmas Fayre. Led by the Abbot and priesthood of the Stationeri, they worshipped—in a polite, easygoing sort of way, so as

* Nome generations, that is. Nomes live ten times faster than humans. To them, ten years is a long lifetime.

not to upset him—Arnold Bros. (est. 1905), who they believed had created everything, i.e., the Store and all the contents therein.

Some families of nomes had grown rich and powerful and took the names—more or less—of the Store departments they lived under . . . the Del Icatessen, the Ironmongri, the Haberdasheri.

And into the Store, on the back of a truck, came the last nomes to live Outside. They knew what wind and rain were, all right. That's why they tried to leave them behind.

Among them was Masklin, rat hunter, and Granny Morkie, and Grimma, although they were women and didn't really count. And, of course, the Thing.

No one quite understood the Thing. Masklin's people had handed it down for centuries; it was very important, that was all they knew. When it came near the electricity in the Store it was able to talk. It *said* it was a thinking machine from a ship which, thousands of years before, had brought the nomes from a far Store, or possibly star. It also said it could hear electricity talk, and one of the things the electricity was saying was that the Store would be demolished in three weeks.

It was Masklin who suggested that the nomes leave the Store on a truck. He found, oddly enough, that actually working out how you could drive a giant truck was the easiest part. The hardest part was getting people to believe that they could do it.

He wasn't the leader. He'd have liked to be a leader. A leader could stick his chin out and do brave things. What Masklin had to do was argue and persuade and, sometimes, lie very slightly. He found it was often easier to get people to do things if you let them think it was their idea.

Ideas! That was the tricky bit, all right. And there were lots of ideas that they needed. They needed to learn to work together. They needed to learn to read. They needed to think that female nomes were, well, nearly as intelligent as males (although everyone knew that really this was ridiculous and that if females were encouraged to think too much their brains would overheat).

Anyway, it all worked. The truck did leave just before the Store mysteriously burned down, and hardly damaging anything very much, it was driven out into the country.

The nomes found an abandoned quarry tucked into a hillside, and moved into the ruined buildings.

And then they knew everything was going to be All Right. There was going to be, they'd heard, a Bright New Dawn.

Whatever *that* was.

Most nomes had never seen a dawn, bright or otherwise, and if they had they would have known that the trouble with bright new dawns is that they're usually followed by cloudy days. With scattered showers.

Six months passed . . .

* * *

This is the story of the Winter.

This is the story of the Great Battle.

This is the story of the awakening of the Cat, the Dragon in the Hill, with eyes like great eyes and a voice like a great voice and teeth like great teeth.

But the story didn't end there.

It didn't start there, either.

The sky blew a gale. The sky blew a fury. The wind became a wall sweeping across the country, a giant stamping on the land. Small trees bent, big trees broke. The last leaves of autumn whirred through the air like lost bullets.

The garbage dump by the gravel pits was deserted. The seagulls that patrolled it had found shelter somewhere, but it was still full of movement. The wind tore into the heaps as though it had something particular against old detergent boxes and leftover shoes. Tin cans rolled into the ruts and clanked miserably, while lighter bits of rubbish flew up and joined the riot in the sky.

Still the wind burrowed. Papers rustled for a while, then got caught and blasted away.

Finally one piece that had been flapping for hours tears free and flies up into the booming air. It looks like a large white bird with oblong wings.

Watch it tumble. . . .

It gets caught on a fence, but very briefly. Half of

it tears off, and now that much lighter, it pinwheels across the furrows of the field beyond. . . .

It is just gathering speed when a hedge looms up and snaps it out of the air like a fly.

One

I. And in that time were Strange Happenings: the Air moved harshly, the Warmth of the Sky grew Less, on some mornings the tops of puddles grew Hard and Cold.

II. And the nomes said unto one another, What is this Thing?

—From the *Book of Nome, Quarries I, v. I–II*

"Winter," said Masklin firmly. "It's called winter."

Abbott Gurder frowned at him.

"You never said it would be like *this*," he said. "It's so *cold*."

"Call this cold?" said Granny Morkie. "Cold? This ain't cold. You think this is cold? You wait till it gets really cold!" She was enjoying this, Masklin noticed; Granny Morkie always enjoyed doom. "It'll be really cold then, when it gets cold. You get *real* frosts, and water comes down out of the sky in frozen bits!" She leaned back triumphantly. "What d'you think of that, then? Eh?"

"You don't have to use baby talk to us," sighed
Gurder. "We *can* read, you know. We know what
snow is."

"Yes," said Dorcas. "There used to be cards with
pictures on them, back in the Store. Every time
Christmas Fayre came around. We know about
snow. It's glittery."

"You get robins," agreed Gurder.

"There's, er, actually there's a bit more to it than
that," Masklin began.

Dorcas waved him into silence. "I don't think we
need to worry," he said. "We're well dug in, the
food stores are looking good, and we know where
to go to get more if we need it. Unless anyone's got
anything else to raise, why don't we close the meeting?"

Everything was going well. Or, at least, not very
badly. That sort of thing always worried Masklin.

Oh, there was still plenty of squabbling and
feuds between the various families, but that was
nomish nature for you. That's why they'd set up
the council, which seemed to be working.

Nomes liked arguing. At least the Council of
Drivers meant they could argue without hitting
one another hardly ever.

Funny thing, though. Back in the Store the great
departmental families had run things. But now all
the families were mixed up and, anyway, there
were no departments in a quarry. But by instinct,
almost, nomes liked hierarchies. The world had al-

ways been neatly divided between those who told people what to do, and those who did it. So, in a strange way, a new set of leaders was emerging.

The Drivers.

It depended on where you had been during the Long Drive. If you were one of the ones who had been in the truck cab, then you were a Driver. Everyone else was just a Passenger. No one talked about it much. It wasn't official or anything. It was just that the bulk of nomekind felt that anyone who could get the Truck all the way here was the sort of person who knew what they were doing.

Being a Driver wasn't necessarily much fun.

Last year, before they'd found the Store, Masklin had to hunt all day. Now he only hunted when he felt like it; the younger Store nomes liked hunting, and apparently it wasn't *right* for a Driver to do it. And they mined potatoes and there'd been a big harvest of corn from a nearby field, even after the machines had been around. Masklin would have preferred the nomes to grow their own food, but they didn't seem to have the knack of making seeds grow in the rock-hard ground of the quarry. But they were getting fed, that was the main thing.

Around him he could feel thousands of nomes living their lives. Raising families. *Settling down.*

He wandered back to his own burrow, down under one of the derelict quarry sheds. After a while he reached a decision and pulled the Thing out of its own hole in the wall.

None of its lights was on. They wouldn't do that

until the Thing was close to electrical wires; then it would light up and be able to talk. There were some wires in the quarry, and Dorcas had got them working. Masklin hadn't taken the Thing to them, though. The solid black box had a way of talking that always made him feel unsettled.

He was pretty certain it could hear, though.

"Old Torrit died last week," he said after a while. "We were a bit sad, but after all, he was very old and he just died. I mean, nothing ate him first or ran him over or anything."

Masklin's little tribe had lived in a highway embankment beside rolling countryside which was full of things that were hungry for fresh nome. The idea that you could die simply of not being alive anymore was a new one to them.

"So we buried him up on the edge of the potato field, too deep for the plow. The Store nomes haven't got the hang of burial yet, I think. They think he's going to sprout, or something. I think they're mixing it up with what you do with seeds. Of course, they don't know about growing things. Because of living in the Store, you see. It's all new to them. They're always complaining about eating food that comes out of the ground, they think it's not natural. And they think the rain is a sprinkler system. I think *they* think the whole world is just a bigger Store. Um."

He stared at the unresponsive cube for a while, scraping his mind for other things to say.

"Anyway, that means Granny Morkie is the oldest nome," he said eventually. "And *that* means she's entitled to a place on the council, even though she's a woman. Abbot Gurder objected to that, but we said, all right, you tell her, and he wouldn't, so she is. Um."

He looked at his fingernails. The Thing had a way of listening that was quite off-putting.

"Everyone's worried about the winter. Um. But we've got masses of potatoes stored up, and it's quite warm down here. The Store nomes have some funny ideas, though. They said that when it was Christmas Fayre time in the Store there was this thing that came called Santer Claws. I just hope it hasn't followed us, that's all. Um."

He scratched an ear.

"All in all, everything's going right. Um."

He leaned closer.

"You know what that means? If you think every-thing's going right, something's going wrong that you haven't heard about yet. That's what I say. Um."

The black cube managed to look sympathetic.

"Everyone says I worry too much. I don't think it's *possible* to worry too much. Um."

He thought some more.

"Um. I think that's about all the news for now." He lifted the Thing up and put it back in its hole.

He'd wondered whether to tell it about his argu-ment with Grimma, but that was, well, personal.

It was all that reading books, that was what it was. He shouldn't have let her learn to read, filling her head with stuff she didn't need to know. Gurder was right, women's brains *did* overheat. Grimma's seemed to be boiling hot the whole time, these days.

He'd gone and said, Look, now everything was settled down more, it was time they got married like the Store nomes did, with the Abbot muttering words and everything.

And she'd said she wasn't sure.

So he'd said, It doesn't work like that, you get told, you get married, that's how it's done.

And she'd said, Not anymore.

He'd complained to Granny Morkie. You'd have expected some support there, he thought. She was a great one for tradition, was Granny. He'd said, Granny, Grimma isn't doing what I tell her.

And *she'd* said, Good luck to her, wish I'd thought of not doin' what I was told when I was a gel.

Then he'd complained to Gurder, who said, Yes, it was very wrong, girls should do what they were instructed. And Masklin had said, Right then, you tell her. And Gurder had said, Well, er, she's got a real temper on her, perhaps it would be better to leave it a bit and these were, after all, changing times. . . .

Changing times. Well, that was true enough. Masklin had done most of the changing. He'd had to make people think in different ways to leave the Store. Changing was necessary. Change was right. He was all in favor of change.

What he was dead against was things not staying the same.

His spear was leaning in the corner. What a pathetic thing it was . . . now. Just a bit of flint held onto the shaft with a twist of binder twine. They'd brought saws and things from the Store. They could use metal these days.

He stared at the spear for some time. Then he picked it up and went out for a long, serious think about things and his position in them. Or, as other people would have put it, a good sulk.

The old quarry was about halfway up the hillside. There was a steep turf slope above it, which in turn became a riot of bramble and hawthorn thicket. There were fields beyond.

Below the quarry a dirt road wound down through scrubby hedges and joined the main highway. Beyond that there was the railroad, another name for two long lines of metal on big wooden blocks. Things like very long trucks went along it sometimes, all joined together.

The nomes had not got the railroad fully worked out yet. But it was obviously dangerous, because they could see a road that crossed it and, whenever the railroad moving thing was coming, two gates came down over the road.

The nomes knew what gates were for. You saw them on fields, to stop things from getting out. It stood to reason, therefore, that the gates were to stop the trains from escaping from their rails and rushing around the place.

Then there were more fields, some gravel pits— good for fishing, for the nomes who wanted fish— and then there was the airport.

Masklin had spent hours in the summer watching the planes. They drove along the ground, he noticed, and then went up sharply, like a bird, and got smaller and smaller and disappeared.

That was the *big* worry. Masklin sat on his favorite stone, in the rain that was starting to fall, and started to worry about it. So many things were worrying him these days he had to stack them up, but below all of them was this big one.

They should be going where the planes went. That was what the Thing had told him, when it was still speaking to him. The nomes had come from the sky. Up above the sky, in fact, which was a bit hard to understand, because surely the only thing there was above the sky was more sky. And they should go back. It was their . . . something beginning with D. Density. Their density. Worlds of their own, they once had. And somehow they'd got stuck here. But—this was the worrying part— the ship thing, the airplane that flew through the really high sky, between the stars, was still up there somewhere. The first nomes had left it behind when they came down here in a smaller ship, and the small ship had crashed, and they hadn't been able to get back.

And he was the only one that knew.

The old Abbot—the one before Gurder—he had known. Grimma and Dorcas and Gurder all knew some of it, but they had busy minds and they were practical people and there was so much to organize these days.

It was just that everyone was settling down. We're going to turn this into our little world, just like in the Store. They thought the roof was the sky, and we think the sky is the roof.

We'll just stay and . . .

There was a truck coming up the quarry road. It was such an unusual sight that Masklin realized he had been watching it for a while without really seeing it at all.

"There was no one on watch! Why wasn't there anyone on watch? I said there should always be someone on watch!"

Half a dozen nomes scurried through the dying bracken toward the quarry gate.

"It was Sacco's turn," muttered Angalo.

"No it wasn't!" hissed Sacco. "You remember, yesterday you asked me to swap because—"

"I don't care whose turn it was!" shouted Masklin. "There was no one there! And there should have been! Right?"

"Sorry, Masklin."

"Yeah. Sorry, Masklin."

They scrambled up a bank and flattened themselves behind a tuft of dried grass.

It was a small truck, as far as trucks went. A

human had already climbed out of it and was doing something to the gates leading into the quarry.

"It's a Land-Rover," said Angalo smugly. He'd spent a long time in the Store reading everything he could about vehicles, before the Long Drive. He liked them. "It's not really a truck, it's more to carry humans over—"

"That human is sticking something on the gate," said Masklin.

"On *our* gate," said Sacco disapprovingly.

"Bit odd," said Angalo. The man sleepwalked, in the slow, ponderous way that humans did, back to the vehicle. Eventually it backed around and roared off.

"All the way up here just to stick a bit of paper on the gate," said Angalo, as the nomes stood up. "That's humans for you."

Masklin frowned. Humans were big and stupid, that was true enough, but there was something unstoppable about them and they seemed to be controlled by bits of paper. Back in the Store a piece of paper had said the Store was going to be demolished and, sure enough, it *had* been demolished. You couldn't trust humans with bits of paper.

He pointed to the rusty wire netting, an easy climb for an agile nome.

"Sacco," he said, "you'd better fetch it down."

Miles away, another piece of paper fluttered on the hedge. Spots of rain pattered across its sun-bleached words, soaking the paper until it was heavy and soggy and . . .

   . . . it tore.

   It flopped onto the grass, free. A breeze made it rustle.

Two

III.   But there came a Sign, *and* people said,
         What is it that this means?
IV.   And it was not good.
                    —From the *Book of Nome, Signs I, v. III–IV*

Gurder shuffled on hands and knees across the paper from the gate.

"Of course I can read it," he said. "I know what every word means."

"Well, then?" said Masklin.

Gurder looked embarrassed. "It's what every sentence means that's giving me trouble," he said. "It says here . . . where was it . . . yes, it says here the quarry is going to be reopened. What does that mean? It's open already, any fool knows that. You can see for miles."

The other nomes crowded around. You certainly could see for miles. That was the terrible part. On three sides the quarry had decently high cliff walls, but on the fourth side . . . well, you got into the habit of not looking in that direction. There was too much of nothing, which made you feel even smaller and more vulnerable than you were already.

Even if the meaning of the paper wasn't clear, it certainly looked unpleasant.

"The quarry's a hole in the ground," said Dorcas. "You can't open a hole unless it's been filled in. Stands to reason."

"A quarry's a place you get stone from," said Grimma. "Humans do it. They dig a hole and they use the stone for making, well, roads and things."

"I expect you read that, did you?" said Gurder sourly. He suspected Grimma of lack of respect for authority. It was also incredibly annoying that, against all the obvious deficiencies of her sex, she was better at reading than he was.

"I did, actually," said Grimma, tossing her head.

"But, you see," said Masklin patiently, "there aren't any more stones here, Grimma. That's why there's a hole."

"Good point," said Gurder, sternly.

"Then he'll make the hole bigger!" snapped Grimma. "Look at those cliffs up there"—they obediently looked—"they're made of stone! Look here"—every head swivelled down to where her foot was tapping impatiently at the paper—"it says it's for a highway extension! He's going to make the quarry bigger! Our quarry! That's what it says he's going to do!"

There was a long silence.

Then Dorcas said, "Who is?"

"Order! He's put his name on it," said Grimma.

"She's right, you know," said Masklin. "Look. It says: To be reopened, by Order."

The nomes shuffled their feet. Order. It didn't sound a promising name. Anyone called Order would probably be capable of anything.

Gurder stood up and brushed the dust off his robe.

"It's only a piece of paper, when all's said and done," he said sullenly.

"But the human came up here," said Masklin. "They've never come up here before."

"Dunno about that," said Dorcas. "I mean, all the quarry buildings. The old workshops. The doorways and so on. I mean, they're for humans. Always worried me, that has. Where humans have been before, they tend to go again. They're rascals for that."

There was another crowded silence, the kind that gets made by lots of people thinking unhappy thoughts.

"Do you mean," said a nome slowly, "that we've come all this way, we've worked so hard to make a place to live in, and now it's going to be taken away?"

"I don't think we should get too disturbed right at this—" Gurder began.

"We've got families here," said another nome. Masklin realized that it was Angalo. He'd been married in the spring to a young lady from the Del

Icatessen family, and they'd already got a fine pair of youngsters, two months old and talking already.

"And we were going to have another go at planting seeds," said another nome. "We've spent ages clearing that ground behind the big sheds. You *know* that."

Gurder raised his hand imploringly.

"We don't know anything," he said. "We mustn't start getting upset until we've found out what's going on."

"And *then* can we get upset?" said another nome sourly. Masklin recognised Nisodemus, one of the Stationeri and Gurder's own assistant. He'd never liked the young nome, and the young nome had never liked anyone, as far as Masklin could see. "I've never, um, been happy with the *feel* of this place, um, I *knew* there was going to be trouble—"

"Now, now, Nisodemus," said Gurder. "There's no cause to go talking like that. We'll have another meeting of the council," he added. "That's what we'll do."

The crumpled newspaper lay beside the road. Occasionally a breeze would blow it randomly along the verge, while a few inches away, the traffic thundered past.

A stronger gust hit at the same time as a particularly large truck roared by, dragging a tail of whirling air. The paper shot up over the road, spread out like a sail, and rose on the wind.

* * *

The Quarry Council was in session, in the space under the floor of the old quarry office.

Other nomes had crowded in and the rest of the tribe milled around outside.

"Look," said Angalo, "there's a big old barn up on the hill, the other side of the potato field. It wouldn't hurt to take some stores up there. Make it ready, you know. Just in case. Then if anything *does* happen, we've got somewhere to go."

"The quarry buildings don't have spaces under the floors, except in the canteen and the office," said Dorcas gloomily. "It's not like the Store. There aren't many places to hide. We need the sheds. If humans come here, we'll have to leave."

"So the barn will be a good idea, won't it?" repeated Angalo.

"There's a human on a tractor who goes up there sometimes," said Masklin.

"We could keep out of its way. Anyway," said Angalo, looking around at the rows of faces, "maybe the humans will go away again. P'raps they'll just take their stone and go. And we can come back. We could send someone to spy on them every day."

"It seems to me you've been thinking about this barn for some time," said Dorcas.

"Me and Masklin talked about it one day when we were hunting up there," said Angalo. "Didn't we, Masklin?"

"Hmm?" said Masklin, who was staring into space.

"You remember, we went up there and I said, 'That'd be a useful place if ever we needed it,' and you said 'Yes.'"

"Hmm," said Masklin.

"Yes, but there's this Winter thing coming," said one of the nomes. "You know. Cold. Glitter on everythin'."

"Robins," another nome put in.

"Yeah," said the first nome uncertainly. "Them too. Not a good time to go movin' around, with robins zoomin' about."

"Nothing wrong with robins," said Granny Morkie, who had nodded off for a moment. "My dad used to say there's good eatin' on a robin, if you catched one." She beamed at them, proudly.

This comment had the same effect on everyone's train of thought as a brick wall built across the line. Eventually Gurder said, "I still say we shouldn't get too excited right at this moment. We should wait and trust in Arnold Bros. (est. 1905)'s guidance."

There was more silence. Then Angalo said, very quietly, "Fat lot of good that'll do us."

There was silence again. But this time it was a thick, heavy silence, and it got thicker and heavier and more menacing, like a storm cloud building up over a mountain, until the first flash of lightning would come as a relief.

It came.

"What did you say?" said Gurder, slowly.

"Only what everyone's been thinking," said

Angalo. Many of the nomes started to stare at their feet.

"And what do you mean by that?" said Gurder.

"Where *is* Arnold Bros. (est. 1905), then?" said Angalo. "*How* did he help us get out of the Store? Exactly, I mean? He didn't, did he?" Angalo shook a bit, as if even he was terrified to hear himself talking like this. "*We* did it. By learning things. We did it all ourselves. We learned to read books, *your* books, and we found things out and we did things for ourselves."

Gurder jumped to his feet, white with fury. Beside him Nisodemus put his hand over his mouth and looked too shocked to speak.

"Arnold Bros. (est. 1905) goes wherever nomes go!" he shouted.

Angalo swayed backward, but his father had been one of the toughest nomes in the Store and he didn't give in easily.

"You just made that up!" he snorted. "I'm not saying that there wasn't, well, *something* in the Store, but that was the Store and this is here and all we've got is *us*! The trouble is, you Stationeri were so powerful in the Store and just can't bear to give it up!"

Now Masklin stood up.

"Just a moment, you two—" he began.

"So that's all it is, is it?" growled Gurder, ignoring him. "That's the Haberdasheri for you! You always were too proud! Too arrogant for your own good! Drive a truck a little way and we think we know it all, do we? Perhaps we're getting what we deserve, eh?"

"This isn't the time or place for this sort of thing—" Masklin went on.

"That's just a silly threat! Why can't you accept it, you old fool, Arnold Bros. doesn't exist! Use the brains Arnold Bros. gave you, why don't you?"

"If you don't both shut up I'll bang your heads together!"

That seemed to work.

"Right," said Masklin, in a more normal voice. "Now, I think it would be a very good idea if everyone went and got on with—with whatever it is they were getting on with. Because this is no way to make complicated decisions. We all need to think for a while."

The nomes filed out, relieved that it was over. Masklin could hear them arguing outside.

"Not you two," he warned.

"Now, *look*—" said Gurder.

"No, you look, the pair of you!" said Masklin, "Here we are, maybe a big problem looming up, and you start arguing! You both ought to know better! Can't you see you're upsetting people?"

"Well, it's important," muttered Angalo.

"What we should do now," said Masklin sharply, "is have another look at this barn. Can't say I'm happy with the idea, but it might be useful to have a bolthole. Anyway, it'll keep people occupied, and that'll stop them from worrying. How about it?"

"I suppose so," said Gurder, with bad grace. "But—"

"No more buts," said Masklin. "You're acting like idiots. People look up to the pair of you, so you'll set an example. Do you hear?"

They glowered at each other, but they both nodded.

"Right, then," said Masklin. "Now, we'll all go out, and people'll see you've made up, and that'll stop their fretting. *Then* we can start planning."

"But Arnold Bros. (est. 1905) *is* important," said Gurder.

"I daresay," said Masklin as they came out into the daylight of the quarry. The wind was dropping again, leaving the sky a deep cold blue.

"There's no daresay about it," said Gurder.

"Listen," said Masklin, "I don't know whether Arnold Bros. exists, or was in the Store, or just lives in our heads or whatever. What I *do* know is that he isn't just going to drop out of the sky."

All three of them glanced up when he said this. The Store nomes shuddered just a bit. It still took a certain courage to look up at the endless sky when you've been used to nice friendly floorboards, but it was traditional, when you referred to Arnold Bros., to look up. Up was where Management and Accounts had been, back in the Store.

"Funny you should say that. There's something up there," said Angalo.

Something white and vaguely rectangular was

drifting gently through the air, and growing bigger.

"It's just a bit of paper," said Gurder. "Something the wind's blown off the dump."

It definitely got a lot bigger, and turned gently in the air as it tumbled into the quarry.

"I think," said Masklin slowly, as its shadow raced toward him across the ground, "that we'd better stand back a bit—"

It dropped on him.

It was, of course, only paper. But nomes are small and it had fallen quite some way, so the force was enough to knock him over.

What was more surprising were the words he saw as he fell backward. They were: Arnold Bros.

Three

I. And they Sought for a Better Sign from Arnold Bros. (est. 1905), and there was a Sign;

II. And some spake up *saying*, Well, all right, but it is really nothing but a Coincidence;

III. But others said, Even a Coincidence can be a Sign.

—From the *Book of Nome, Signs II, v. I–III*

Masklin had always kept an open mind on the subject of Arnold Bros. (est. 1905). After all, the Store had been pretty impressive, what with the escalators and so on, and if Arnold Bros. (est. 1905) hadn't created it, who had? After all, that only left humans. Not that he considered humans were as stupid as most nomes thought. They might be big and slow but there was a sort of mindless unstoppability about them. They could certainly be taught to do simple tasks.

On the other hand, the world was *miles* across and full of complicated things. It seemed to be asking a lot of Arnold Bros. (est. 1905) to create the whole thing.

So Masklin had decided not to decide anything about Arnold Bros. (est. 1905), in the hope that if there *was* an Arnold Bros. (est. 1905) and he found out about Masklin, he wouldn't mind much.

The trouble with having an open mind, of course, is that people will insist on coming along and trying to put things in it.

The faded newspaper from the sky had been carefully spread out on the floor of one of the old sheds.

It was covered in words. Most of them even Masklin could understand, but even Grimma had to admit she couldn't guess at what they were supposed to mean when you read them all in one go. SCHOOL SLAMS SHOCK PROBE, for example, was a mystery. So was FURY OVER TAXES REBEL. So was PLAY SUPER BINGO IN YOUR SOARAWAY BLACKBURY EVENING POST & GAZETTE. But they were mysteries that would have to wait.

What all eyes were staring at was the quite small area of words, about nome-sized, under the word PEOPLE.

"That means people," said Grimma.

"Really?" said Masklin.

"And the lettering underneath it says: 'Fun-loving, globetrotting millionaire playboy Richard Arnold will be jetting to the Florida sunshine next week to witness the launch of Arnsat 1, the first communi"—she hesitated—"cations sat . . . ellite

· *28* ·

built by the Arnco Inter . . . national Group. This leap into the future comes only a few months after the dest . . . ruction by fire of—"

The nomes, who'd been silently reading along with her, shivered.

"—Arnold Bros., the store here in Blackbury which was the first of the Arnold chain and the basis of the multimillion-pound trad . . . ing group. It was founded in 1905 by Alderman Frank W. Arnold and his brother Arthur. Grand . . . son Richard, 39, who will . . ." Her voice faded to a whisper.

"Grandson Richard, 39," repeated Gurder, his face bright with triumph. "What d'you think of *that*, eh?"

"What does globe-trotting mean?" said Masklin.

"Well, globe means ball, and trotting is a sort of slow running," said Grimma. "So he runs slowly on a ball. Globe-trotting."

"This is a message from Arnold Bros.," said Gurder ponderously. "It's been sent to us. A message."

"A message meant, um, for us!" said Nisodemus, who was standing just behind Gurder. He held up his hands. "Yea, all the way from—"

"Yes, yes, Nisodemus," said Gurder. "Do be quiet, there's a good chap." He gave Masklin an embarrassed look.

"Doesn't sound very likely, running slowly. I mean, you'd fall off. If it was a ball, is what I'm saying," said Masklin.

They stared at the Picture again. It was made up of tiny dots. They showed a smiling face. It had teeth and a beard.

"It stands to reason," said Gurder, more confidently. "Arnold Bros. (est. 1905) has sent Grandson Richard, 39, to . . . to . . ."

"And these two names who founded the Store," said Masklin. "I don't understand that. I thought Arnold Bros. (est. 1905) created the Store."

"Then these two founded it," said Gurder. "That makes sense. It was a big Store. It'd be easy to find, even if you weren't looking for it." He looked slightly uneasy. "Losted and founded," he said, half to himself. "That makes sense. Yes."

"O-kay," said Dorcas. "So let's just see where we've got to. The message is, is it, is that Grandson Richard, 39, is in Florida, wherever that is—"

"Going to *be* in Florida," said Grimma.

"It's a type of colored juice," volunteered a nome. "I know, 'cause one day when we went over to the garbage dump, there was this old carton, and it said Florida Orange Juice. I read it," he added proudly.

"Going to *be* in this orange-colored juice, so I'm given to understand," said Dorcas doubtfully. "Running slowly on a ball and jetting, whatever that is. And liking it, apparently."

The nomes fell silent while they thought about this.

"Holy utterances are often difficult to understand," said Gurder gravely.

"This must be a *powerful* holy one," said Dorcas.

"*I* think it's just a coincidence," said Angalo loftily. "This is just a story about a human being, like in some of the books we read."

"And how many humans could even stand on a ball, let alone run slowly on it?" demanded Gurder.

"All *right*," said Angalo, "But what are we going to *do*, then?"

Gurder's mouth opened and shut a few times. "Why, it's obvious," he said uncertainly.

"Tell us, then." said Angalo sourly.

"Well, er. It's, er, obvious. We must go to, er, the place where the orange juice is . . ."

"Yes?" said Angalo.

"And, er, and find Grandson Richard, 39, which should be easy, you see, because we've got this picture." Gurder scratched his chin. "I mean, how many humans can there *be* in the world?" he said. "Not more than a few hundred. And when we've found him . . ."

"Yes?" said Angalo.

Gurder have him a haughty look. "Remember the commandment that Arnold Bros. (est. 1905) put up in the Store," he said. "Did it not say 'If you do not see what you require, please ask'?"

The nomes nodded. Many of them had seen it. And the other commandments: "Everything Must Go," and, by the escalators, "Dogs and Strollers Must Be Carried." They were the words of Arnold Bros. (est. 1905). You couldn't really argue with them. . . . But on the other hand, well, that had been the Store, and this was here.

"And?" said Angalo.

Gurder began to sweat. "Well, er, and then we ask him to let us be left alone in the quarry."

There was an awkward silence.

Then Angalo said, "That sounds about the most half-baked—"

"What does jetting mean?" said Grimma. "Is it anything to do with jet?"

"A jet is a kind of aircraft," said Angalo, the transport expert.

"So jetting means to go like an aircraft. Or in an aircraft?" said Grimma.

Everyone turned to Masklin, whose fascination with the airport was well known to one and all.

He wasn't there.

Masklin pulled the Thing from its niche in the wall and padded back out into the open. The Thing didn't have to be attached to any wires. It was enough to put it near them.

There was electricity in the old manager's office. He ran across the empty alley between the tumble-down buildings and squeezed his way in through a crack in the sagging door.

Then he placed the box in the middle of the floor and waited.

It always took some while for the Thing to wake up. Its lights flickered at random and it made odd beeping noises. Masklin supposed it was the machine's equivalent of a nome getting up in the morning.

Eventually it said, *"Who is there?"*

"It's me," said Masklin, "Masklin. Look, I need to know what the words 'communications satellite' mean. I've heard you use the word 'satellite' before. You said the Moon is one, didn't you?"

"Yes. But communications satellites are artificial moons. They are used for communications. Communications means the transferring of information. In this case, by radio and television."

"What's television?" said Masklin.

"A means of sending pictures through the air."

"Does this happen a lot?"

"All the time."

Masklin made a mental note to look out for any pictures in the air.

"I see," he lied. "So these satellites—where are they, exactly?"

"In the sky."

"I don't think I've ever seen one," said Masklin doubtfully. There was an idea forming in his mind. He wasn't quite sure yet. Bits and pieces of things he'd read and heard were coming together. The important thing was to let them take their own time, and not frighten them away.

"They are in orbit, many miles up. There are a great many above this planet," said the Thing.

"How do you know that?"

"I can detect them."

"Oh."

Masklin stared at the flickering lights.

"If they are artificial, does that mean they're not real?" he said.

"They are machines. They are usually built on the planet and then launched into space."

The idea was nearly there. It was rising like a bubble.

"Space is where our ship is, you said."

"That is correct."

Masklin felt the idea explode quietly, like a dandelion. "If we knew where one of these things was going to be flown into space," he said, speaking quickly before the words had time to escape, "and we could sort of hang on to the sides or whatever, or maybe drive it like the Truck, and we took you with us, then we could jump off when we got up there and go and find this ship of ours, couldn't we?"

The lights on top of the Thing moved oddly, into patterns Masklin had never seen before. This went on for quite a while before it spoke again. When it did, it sounded almost sad.

"Do you know how big space is?" it said.

"No," said Masklin politely. "It's pretty big, is it?"

"Yes. However, it may be possible for me to detect and summon the ship if I were taken above the atmosphere. But do you know what the words 'oxygen supply' mean?"

"No."

" *'Space suit'?"*

"No."

"It is very cold in space."

"Well, couldn't we sort of jump around a bit to keep warm?" said Masklin desperately.

"I think you do not appreciate what it is that space contains."

"What's that, then?"

"Nothing. It contains nothing. And everything. But there is very little everything and more nothing than you could imagine."

"It's still worth a try, though, isn't it?"

"What you are proposing is an extremely unwise endeavor," said the Thing.

"Yes, but, you see," said Masklin firmly, "if I don't try, then it's always going to be like this. We're always going to escape, and find somewhere new, and just when we're getting the hang of it all, we'll have to go again. Sooner or later we must find somewhere that we can know really belongs to us. Dorcas is right. Humans get everywhere. Anyway, you were the one who told me that our home was . . . up there somewhere."

"This is not the right time. You are ill-prepared."

Masklin clenched his fists. "I'll never be well prepared! I was born in a hole, Thing! A muddy hole in the ground! How can I ever be well prepared for anything? That's what being alive *is*, Thing! It's being badly prepared for everything! Because you only get one chance, Thing! You only get one chance and then you die and they don't let you go around again after you've got the hang of it! Do you understand, Thing! So we'll try it *now*! I *order* you to help! You're a machine and you must do what you're told!"

The lights formed a spiral.

"You're learning fast," said the Thing.

Four

III. And in a voice like Thunder, the Great
Masklin said unto the Thing, Now is the
Time to go back to our Home in the Sky;
IV. Or we will Forever be Running from
Place to Place.
V. But none must know what I intend, or
they will say, Ridiculous, Why go to the
Sky when we Have Problems Right here?
VI. Because that is how People are.
—From the *Book of Nome, Quarries II, v. III–VI*

Gurder and Angalo were having a blazing row
when Masklin got back.

He didn't try to interrupt. He just put the Thing
down on the floor and sat down next to it, and
watched them.

Funny how people needed to argue. The whole
secret was not to listen to what the other person
was saying, Masklin had noticed.

Gurder and Angalo had really got the hang of
that. The trouble was that neither of them was en-

tirely certain he was right, and the funny thing was that people who weren't *entirely* certain they were right always argued much louder than other people, as if the main person they were trying to convince was themselves. Gurder was not certain, not *entirely* certain, that Arnold Bros. (est. 1905) really existed, and Angalo wasn't entirely certain that he didn't.

Eventually Angalo noticed Masklin.

"You tell him, Masklin," he said. "He wants to go and find Grandson Richard, 39!"

"Do you? Where do you think we should look?" Masklin asked Gurder.

"The airport," said Gurder. "You know that. Jetting. In a jet. That's what he'll do."

"But we *know* the airport!" said Angalo. "I've been right up to the fence several times! Humans go in and out of it all day! Grandson Richard, 39, looks just like them! He could have gone already. He could be in the juice by now! You can't believe words that just drop out of the sky!" He turned to Masklin again. "Masklin's a steady lad," he said, "he'll tell you. You tell him, Masklin," he said. "You listen to him, Gurder. He thinks about things, Masklin does. At a time like this—"

"Let's go to the airport," said Masklin.

"There," said Angalo, "I told you, Masklin isn't the kind of nome—what?"

"Let's go to the airport and watch."

Angalo's mouth opened and shut silently.

"But . . . but . . ." he managed.

"It must be worth a try," said Masklin.

"But it's all just a coincidence!" said Angalo.

Masklin shrugged. "Then we'll come back. I'm not suggesting we *all* go. Just a few of us."

"But supposing something happens while we're gone?"

"It'll happen anyway, then. There's thousands of us. Getting people to the old barn won't be difficult, if we need to do it. It's not like the Long Drive."

Angalo hesitated.

"Then *I'll* go," he said. "Just to prove to you how . . . how superstitious you're being."

"Good," said Masklin.

"Provided Gurder comes, of course," Angalo added.

"What?" said Gurder.

"Well, you *are* the Abbot," said Angalo sarcastically. "If we're going to talk to Grandson Richard, 39, then it'd better be you. I mean, he probably won't want to listen to anyone else."

"Aha!" shouted Gurder. "You think I won't come! It'd be worth it just to see your face—"

"That's settled, then," said Masklin calmly. "And now, I think we'd better see about keeping a special watch on the road. And some teams had better go to the old barn. And it would be a good idea to see what people can carry. Just in case, you know."

* * *

Grimma was waiting for him outside. She didn't look happy.

"I know you," she said. "I know the kind of expression you have when you're getting people to do things they don't want to do. What are you planning?"

They strolled into the shadow of a rusting sheet of corrugated iron. Masklin occasionally squinted upward. This morning he'd thought the sky was just a blue thing with clouds. Now it was something that was full of words and invisible pictures and machines whizzing around. Why was it that the more you found out, the less you really *knew*?

Eventually he said, "I can't tell you. I'm not quite sure myself."

"It's to do with the Thing, isn't it?"

"Yes. Look, if I'm away for, er, a little bit longer than—"

She stuck her hands on her hips. "I'm not stupid, you know," she said. "Orange-colored juice, indeed! I've read nearly every book we brought out of the Store. Florida is a . . . a *place*. Just like the quarry. Probably even bigger. And it's a long way away. You have to go across a lot of water to get there."

"I think it might even be further away than we came on the Long Drive," said Masklin quietly. "I know, because one day when we went to look at the airport I saw water on the other side, by the road. It looked as though it went on forever."

"I told you," said Grimma smugly. "It was probably an ocean."

"There was a sign by it," said Masklin. "Can't remember everything on it. I'm not as good at the reading as you. One of the words was . . . res-er-voir, I think."

"There you are, then."

"But it must be worth a try." Masklin scowled. "There's only one place where we can ever be safe, and that's where we belong," he said. "Otherwise we'll always have to keep running away."

"Well, I don't like it," said Grimma.

"But *you* said you didn't like running away," said Masklin. "There isn't an alternative, is there? Let me just try something. If it doesn't work, then we'll come back."

"But supposing something goes wrong? Supposing you don't come back? I'll . . ." Grimma hesitated.

"Yes?" said Masklin hopefully.

"I'll have a terrible job explaining things to people," she said firmly. "It's a silly idea. I don't want to have anything to do with it."

"Oh." Masklin looked disappointed but defiant. "Well, I'm going to try anyway. Sorry."

Five

V.   And he said, What are these frogs of which you speak?
VI. And she said, You wouldn't understand.
VII. And he said, You are right.
—From the *Book of Nome, Strange Frogs I, v. V–VII*

There was a busy night . . .

It would be a journey of several hours to the barn. Parties went on to mark the path and generally prepare the way, besides watching out for foxes. Not that they were often seen, these days; a fox might be quite happy to attack a solitary nome, but thirty well-armed, enthusiastic hunters were a different proposition, and it would be a very stupid fox indeed that even showed an interest. The few that did live near the quarry tended to wander off hurriedly in the opposite direction whenever they saw a nome. They'd learned that nomes meant trouble.

It had been a hard lesson for some of them. Not long after the nomes moved into the quarry a fox was surprised and delighted to come across a couple of unwary berry gatherers, which it ate. It was even more surprised that night when two hundred grim-faced nomes tracked it to its den, lit a fire in the entrance, and speared it to death when it ran out, eyes streaming.

There were a lot of animals that would like to dine off nome, Masklin had said. They'd better learn: it's us or them. And they'd better learn right now that it's going to be *them*. No animal is going to get a taste for nome. Not anymore.

"Of course it might all be nothing to worry about," said Angalo nervously, around dawn. "We might never have to move."

"Just when we were beginning to get settled down, too," said Dorcas. "Still, I reckon that if we keep a proper lookout we can have everyone on the move in five minutes. And we'll start moving some food stores up there this morning. No harm in that. Then they'll be there if we need them."

Nomes sometimes went as far as the airport. There was a garbage dump on the way, which was a prime source of bits of cloth and wire, and the flooded gravel pits further on were handy if anyone had the patience to fish. It was a pleasant enough day's journey, largely along badger tracks. There was a main road to be crossed, or rather, to be burrowed under; for some reason pipes had been carefully put underneath it just where the track needed to cross it. Presumably the badgers had done it. They certainly used it a lot.

Masklin found Grimma in her schoolhole under one of the old sheds, supervising a class in writing. She glared at him, told the children to get on with it—and would Nicco Haberdasheri like to share the joke with the rest of the class? No? Then he could jolly well get on with things—and came out into the passage.

"I've just called to say we're off," said Masklin, twiddling his hat in his hands. "There's a load of nomes going over to the dump, so we'll have company the rest of the way. Er."

"Electricity," said Grimma, vaguely.

"What?"

"There's no electricity at the old barn," said Grimma. "You remember what that meant? On moonless nights there was nothing to do but stay in the burrow. I don't want to go back to that."

"Well, maybe we were better nomes for it," mumbled Masklin. "We didn't have all the things we've got today, but we were—"

"Cold, frightened, ignorant, and hungry!" snapped Grimma. "You know that. You try telling Granny Morkie about the Good Old Days and see what she says."

"We had each other," said Masklin.

Grimma examined her hands.

"We were just the same age and living in the same hole," she said vaguely. She looked up. "But it's all different now! There . . . well, there are the frogs, for one thing."

Masklin looked blank. And, for once, Grimma looked unsure.

"I read about them in a book," she said. "There's this place, you see. Called South America. And there are these hills where it's hot and rains all the time, and in the rain forests there are these very tall trees and right in the top branches of the trees there are these, like, great big flowers called bromeliads and water gets into the flowers and makes little pools and there's a type of frog that lays eggs in the pools and tadpoles hatch and grow into new frogs and these little frogs live their whole lives in the flowers right at the top of the trees and don't even know about the ground and the world is full of things like that and now I know about them and I'm never ever going to be able to see them, and then *you*, " she gulped for breath, "want me to come and live with you in a hole and wash your socks!"

Masklin ran this sentence through his head again, in case it made any sense when he listened to it a second time.

"But I don't wear socks," he pointed out.

This was apparently not the right thing to say. Grimma prodded him in the stomach.

"Masklin," she said, "you're a good nome and bright enough in your way, but there aren't any answers up in the sky. You need to have your feet on the ground, not your head in the air!"

She swept away and shut the door behind her.

Masklin felt his ears growing hot.

"I can do both!" Masklin shouted after her. "At the same time!"

He thought about it and added, "So can everyone!"

He stamped off along the tunnel. Bright enough in his way! Gurder was right, universal education was not a good idea. He'd never understand women, he thought. Even if he lived to be ten.

Gurder had turned over the leadership of the Stationeri to Nisodemus. Masklin felt less than happy about this. It wasn't that Nisodemus was stupid. Quite the reverse. He was clever in a bubbling, sideways way that Masklin distrusted; he always seemed to be bottling up excitement about something, and when he spoke the words always rushed out, with Nisodemus putting "ums" in the flow of words so that he could catch his breath without anyone having the chance to interrupt him. He made Masklin uneasy. He mentioned this to Gurder.

"Nisodemus might be a bit overenthusiastic," said Gurder, "but his heart's in the right place."

"What about his head?"

"Listen," said Gurder. "We know each other well enough, don't we? We understand one another, wouldn't you say?"

"Yes. Why?"

"Then I'll let you make the decisions that affect all nomes' bodies," said Gurder, his voice just one step away from being threatening, "and you'll let me make the decisions that affect all nomes' souls. Fair enough?"

And so they set off.

The good-byes, the last-minute messages, the organization, and, because they were nomes, the hundred little arguments, are not important.

They set off.

Life at the quarry began to get back to something like normal. No more trucks came up to the gate. Dorcas sent a couple of his more agile young assistant engineers up the wire netting, just in case, to stuff the rusty padlock full of mud. He also ordered a team of nomes to twist wire around and around the gates as well.

"Not that it'd hold them very long," he said. "Not if they were determined."

The council, or what was left of it now, nodded wisely, although frankly none of them understood or cared much about mechanical things.

The truck came back the same afternoon. The two nomes watching the truck hurried back into the quarry to report. The driver had fiddled with the padlock for a while, pulled at the wire, and then driven off.

"And it said something," said Sacco.

"Yes, it said something. Sacco heard it," said his partner, Nooty Kiddies-Klothes. She was a plump young nome who wore trousers and was good at engineering and had actually volunteered to be a guard instead of staying at home learning how to cook; things were really changing in the quarry.

"I heard it say something," said Sacco helpfully, in case the point hadn't sunk in.

"That's right," said Nooty. "We both heard it, didn't we, Sacco?"

"And what was it?" said Dorcas encouragingly. I don't really deserve this sort of thing, he thought. Not at my time of life. I'd rather be in my workshop, trying to get this radio business sorted out.

"It said," Sacco took a deep breath, his eyes bulged, and he attempted the foghorn mooing that was human sound, " 'Bbblllloooooooooddddyyy kkiiiddddddssss!' "

Dorcas looked at the others.

"Anyone got any ideas?" he said. "It almost seems to mean something, doesn't it? I tell you, if only we could understand them—"

"This must have been one of the stupid ones," said Nooty. "It was trying to get in!"

"Then it'll come back," said Dorcas gloomily. He shook his head.

"All right, you two," he said. "Well done. Get back on watch. Thank you."

He watched them go off hand in hand, and then he wandered away across the quarry, heading for the old manager's office.

I've seen Christmas Fayre come around six times, he thought. That's six whatd'youcall'ems, years. And almost one more, I think, although it's hard to be sure out here. No one puts up any signs to say what's happening, the heating just gets turned down. Seven years old. Just about the time when a nome ought to be taking it easy. And I'm out here, where there aren't any proper walls to the world, and the water goes cold and hard as glass some mornings, and the ventilation and heating systems are quite shockingly out of control. Of course—he pulled himself together a bit—as a scientist I find all these phenomena extremely interesting. It would just be nicer to find them extremely interesting from somewhere nice and snug, inside.

Ah, inside. That was the place to be. Most of the older nomes suffered from the fear of the Outside, but no one liked to talk about it much. It wasn't too bad in the quarry, with its great walls of rock. If you didn't look up too much, or look toward the fourth side with its terribly huge views across the countryside, you could almost believe you were back in the Store. Even so, most of the older nomes preferred to stay in the sheds, or in the cozy gloom under the floorboards. That way you avoided this horrible *exposed* feeling, the dreadful sensation that the sky was watching you.

The children seemed to quite like the Outside, though. They weren't really used to anything else. They could just about remember the Store, but it didn't mean much to them. They belonged Outside. They were used to it. And the young men who went out hunting and gathering . . . well, young men liked to show how brave they were, didn't they? Especially in front of other young men. And young women.

Of course, Dorcas thought, as a scientist and rational-thinking nome I know we weren't really intended to live under floorboards the whole time. It's just that, as a nome who is probably seven years old and feeling a bit creaky, I've got to admit I'd find it sort of comforting to have a few of the good old signs around the place. "Amazing Reductions," perhaps, or just a little sign saying, "Mammoth Sales Start Tomorrow." It wouldn't hurt, and I'm sure I'd feel happier. Which is of course totally ridiculous, when you look at it rationally.

It'd just be like Arnold Bros. (est. 1905), he thought sadly. I'm pretty sure he doesn't exist in the way I was taught he does, when I was young. But when you saw things like "If you do not see what you require, please ask" on the walls, you felt that everything was somehow *all right.*

He thought: These are very wrong thoughts for a rational thinking nome.

There was a crack in the woodwork by the door of the manager's office. Dorcas slipped into the familiar gloom under the floor and padded along until he found the switch.

He was rather proud of this idea. There was a big red bell on the outside wall of the office, presumably so that humans could hear the telephone ring when the quarry was noisy. Dorcas had changed the wiring so that he could make it ring whenever he liked.

He pressed the switch.

Nomes came running from all corners of the quarry. Dorcas waited as the underfloor space filled up, and then dragged up an empty matchbox to stand on.

"The human has been back," he announced. "It didn't get in, but it'll keep trying."

"What about your wire?" said one of the nomes.

"I'm afraid there are such things as wire cutters."

"So much for your theory about, um, humans being intelligent. A *intelligent* human would know enough not to go, um, where it wasn't wanted," said Nisodemus sourly.

Dorcas liked to see eagerness in a young nome, but Nisodemus vibrated with a peculiarly hungry kind of eagerness that was unpleasant to see. He gave him as sharp a look as he dared.

"Humans out here might be different from the ones in the Store," he snapped. "Anyway—"

"Order must have sent it," said Nisodemus. "It's a judgment, um, on us!"

"None of that. It's just a human," said Dorcas. Nisodemus glared at him as he went on, "Now, we really should be sending some of the women and children to the—"

There was the sound of running feet outside and the gate guards piled in through the crack.

"It's back! It's back!" panted Sacco. "The human's back!"

"All right, all right," said Dorcas. "Don't worry about it, it can't—"

"No! No! No!" yelled Sacco, jumping up and down. "It's got a pair of cutter things! It's cut the wire *and* the chain that holds the gates shut and it—"

They didn't hear the rest of it.

They didn't need to.

The sound of an engine coming closer said it all.

It grew so loud that the shed shook, and then it stopped suddenly, leaving a nasty kind of silence that was worse than the noise. There was the crump of a metal door slamming. Then the rattle and squeak of the shed door.

Then footsteps. The boards overhead buckled and dropped little clouds of dust as the great thumping steps wandered around the office.

The nomes stood in absolute silence. They moved nothing except their eyes, but *they* moved in perfect time to the footsteps, marking the position, flicking backward and forward as the human crossed the room above. A baby started to whimper.

There was some clicking, and then the muffled sound of a human voice making its usual incomprehensible noises. This went on for some time.

Then the footsteps left the office again. The nomes could hear them crunching around outside, and then more noises. Nasty, clinking metal noises.

A small nome said, "Mom, I want to go, Mom—"

"Shh!"

"I really *mean* it, Mom!"

"Will you be quiet!"

All the nomes stood stock-still as the noises went on around them. Well, nearly all. One small nome hopped from one foot to the other, going very red in the face.

Eventually the noise stopped. There was the thunk of a truck door closing, the growl of its engine, and the motor noise died away.

Dorcas said, very quietly, "I think perhaps we can relax now."

Hundreds of nomes breathed a sigh of relief.

"Mom!"

"Yes, all right, off you go."

And after the sigh of relief, the outbreak of babble. One voice rose above the rest.

"It was never like this in the Store!" said Nisodemus, climbing onto half a brick. "I ask you, fellow nomes, is this what we were led, um, to expect?"

There was a mumbled chorus of "nos" and "yesses" as Nisodemus went on. "A year ago we were safe in the Store. Do you remember what it was like at Christmas Fayre? Do you remember what it was like in the Food Hall? Anyone remember, um, roast beef and turkey?"

There were one or two embarrassed cheers. Nisodemus looked triumphant. "And here we are at the same time of year—well, *they* tell us it's the same time of year," he said sarcastically, "and what we're expected to eat are knobbly things actually grown in *dirt*! Um. And the meat isn't proper meat at all, it's just dead animals cut up! Actual dead animals, actually cut up! Is this what you want your, um, children to get used to? Digging up their food? And *now* they tell us we might even have to go to some barn that hasn't got proper floorboards for us to live under as Arnold Bros. (est. 1905) intended. Where next? we ask ourselves. Out in a field somewhere? Um. And do you know what is the worst thing about all of this? I'll tell you." He pointed a finger at Dorcas. "The people who seem to be giving us all the orders now are the very people who, um, got us into this trouble in the first place!"

"Now, just you hold on—" Dorcas began.

"You all know I'm right!" shouted Nisodemus. "Think about it, nomes! Why in the name of Arnold Bros. (est. 1905) did we have to leave the Store?"

There were a few more vague cheers and several arguments broke out among the audience.

"Don't be stupid," said Dorcas. "The Store was going to be demolished!"

"We don't know that!" shouted Nisodemus.

"Of course we do!" roared Dorcas. "Masklin and Gurder saw—"

"And where are they now, eh?"

"They've gone to . . . well, they've gone to . . ." Dorcas began. He wasn't much good at this, he knew. Why did it have to be him? He preferred messing around with wires and bolts and things. Bolts didn't keep shouting at you.

"Yes, they've gone!" Nisodemus lowered his voice to a sort of angry hiss. "Think about it, you nomes! Use your, um, brains! In the Store we knew where we were, things worked, everything was exactly as Arnold Bros. (est. 1905) decreed. And suddenly we're out here. Remember how you used to despise Outsiders? Well, the Outsiders are us! Um. And now it's all panic again, and it always will be —until we mend our ways and Arnold Bros. (est. 1905) graciously allows us back into the Store as better, wiser nomes!"

"Let's just get this clear," said a nome. "Are you saying that the Abbot *lied* to us?"

"I'm not saying anything like that," said Nisodemus, sniffing. "I'm just presenting you with the facts. Um. That's all I'm doing."

"But . . . but . . . but the Abbot has gone to get help," said a lady nome uncertainly. "And . . . and . . . after all, I'm *sure* the Store was demolished. I mean, we wouldn't have gone to all this trouble otherwise, would we? Er." She looked desperate.

"I know this, though," said the nome beside her, "Say what you like, but I don't fancy this old barn everyone's talking about. There's not even any electric there."

"Yes, and it's in the middle of"—another nome began, and then lowered his voice—"you know. Things. You know what I'm talking about."

"Yeah," said an elderly nome. "*Things.* I've seen 'em. My lad took me blackberryin' a month or two back, up above the quarry, and I seen 'em."

"I don't mind seeing them a long way off," said the worried lady nome. "It's the thought of being in the middle of them that makes me come over all shaky."

They don't even like to say the words *open fields*, thought Dorcas. I know how they feel.

"It's snug enough here, I'll grant you," said the first nome. "But all this stuff you get outside, what d'you call it, begins with an N—"

"Nature?" said Dorcas weakly. Nisodemus was smiling madly, his eyes sparkling.

"That's right," said the nome. "Well, it's not natural. And there's a sight too much of it. 'S not like a proper world at all. You've only got to look at it. The floor's all rough, 'n' it should be flat. There's hardly any walls. All them little starry lights that come out at night, well, they're not much help, are they? And now these humans go where they please, there's no proper regulations like there was in the Store."

"That's why Arnold Bros. established the Store in 1905," said Nisodemus. "A *proper* place for, um, nomes to live."

Dorcas gently grabbed Sacco's ear and pulled the young nome toward him.

"Do you know where Grimma is?" he whispered.

"Isn't she here?"

"I'm quite sure she isn't," said Dorcas. "She'd have had something very sharp to say by now if she was. She may have stayed in the schoolhole with the children when the bell went off. It's just as well."

Nisodemus has something on his mind, he thought. I'm not certain what it is, but it smells bad.

And it got worse as the day wore on, especially since it began to rain. A nasty, freezing sort of rain. Sleet, according to Granny Morkie. It was soggy, not really water but not quite ice. Rain with bones.

Somehow it seemed to find its way into places where ordinary rain hadn't managed to get. Dorcas organized younger nomes to dig drainage trenches and rigged up a few of the big lightbulbs for heat. The older nomes sat hunched around them, sneezing and grumbling.

Granny Morkie did her best to cheer them up. Dorcas began to really wish the old woman wouldn't do that.

"This ain't nothing," she said. "I remember the Great Flood. Made our hole cave right in, we was cold and drenched for days!" She cackled and rocked backward and forward. "Liked drownded rats, we was! Not a dry stitch on, you know, and no fire for a week. Talk about laugh!"

The Store nomes stared at her, and shivered.

"And you don't want to go worrying about crossing them open fields," she went on, conversationally. "Nine times out o' ten you don't get et by anything."

"Oh, dear," said a lady nome, faintly.

"Yes, I've been out in fields hundreds o' times. It's a doddle if you stay close to the hedge and keep your eyes open, you hardly ever have to run very much," said Granny.

No one's temper was improved when they learned that the Land-Rover had parked right on the patch of ground they were going to plant things in. The nomes had spent ages during the summer hacking the hard ground into something resembling soil. They'd even planted seeds, which hadn't grown. Now there were two great ruts in it, and a new padlock and chain on the gate.

The sleet was already filling the ruts. Oil had leaked in and formed a rainbow sheen on the surface.

And all the time Nisodemus was reminding people how much better it had been in the Store. They didn't really need much persuading. After all, it *had* been better. Much better.

I mean, thought Dorcas, we can keep warm and there's plenty of food, although there is a limit to the number of ways you can cook rabbit and potatoes. The trouble is, Masklin thought that once we got outside the Store we'd all be digging and building and hunting and facing the future with strong chins and bright smiles. Some of the youngsters are doing well enough, I'll grant you. But us old 'uns are too set in our ways. It's all right for me, I like tinkering with things, I can be useful, but the rest of them, well . . . all they've really got to occupy themselves is grumbling, and they've become really *good* at that.

I wonder what Nisodemus's game is? He's too keen, if you ask me.

I wish Masklin would come back.

Even young Gurder wasn't too bad.

It's been three days now.

At a time like this, he knew he'd feel better if he went and looked at the Cat.

Six

I.   For in the hill was a Beast, from the days when the World was made.

II.   But it was old and broken and dying.

III. And the mark of its name was on it.

IV. And the mark was the mark of the Cat.

        —From the *Book of Nome, Cat I, v. I–IV*

The Cat.

The Cat was his. His little secret. His *big* secret, really. No one else knew about the Cat, not even Dorcas's assistants.

He'd been pottering around in the big old half-ruined sheds on the other side of the quarry, one day back in the summer. He hadn't really got any aim in mind, except perhaps the possibility of finding a useful bit of wire or something.

So he'd rummaged around in the shadows, straightened up, glanced above him *and there the Cat was.*

With its mouth open.

It had been a terrible few seconds until Dorcas's eyes adjusted to the distance.

After that he'd spent a lot of time with the Cat, poking around, finding out about him. Or *it*. The Cat was too big to be a him or a her, it had to be an *it*. A terrible it, perhaps, and old and wounded, like a dragon that had come here for one last final sleep. Or perhaps it was like one of those big animals Grimma had showed him in a book once. Diner soars.

Dorcas had never seen a cat before, but he'd heard from Masklin that they were dangerous, and Dorcas wasn't about to argue.

But this cat was kind of peaceful to have around. It didn't grumble, and it didn't keep on asking Dorcas why he hadn't got around to inventing radio *yet*. Dorcas had spent many a peaceful hour getting to know the Cat. It was someone to talk to. It was the best kind of person to talk to, in fact, because you didn't have to listen back at it.

Dorcas shook his head. There was no time for that sort of thing now. Everything was going wrong.

Instead, he went to find Grimma. She seemed to have her head screwed on right, even if she was a girl.

The schoolhole was under the floor of the old shed with CANTEEN on the door. It was Grimma's personal world. She'd invented schools for children, on the idea that since reading and writing were quite difficult it was best to get them over with early.

The library was also kept there.

In those last hectic hours the nomes had managed to rescue about thirty books from the Store. Some were very useful—*Gardening All the Year Round* was well thumbed, and Dorcas knew *Essential Theory for the Amateur Engineer* almost by heart —but some were, well, difficult, and not opened much.

Grimma was standing in front of one of these when he wandered in. She was biting her thumb, which she always did when she was concentrating.

He had to admire the way she read. Not only was Grimma the best reader among the nomes, she also had an amazing ability to understand what she was reading.

"Nisodemus is causing trouble," he said, sitting down on a bench.

"I know," said Grimma vaguely. "I've heard." She grabbed the edge of the page in both hands, and turned it over with a grunt of effort.

"I don't know what he's got to gain," said Dorcas.

"Power," said Grimma. "We've got a *power vacuum*, you see."

"I don't think we have," said Dorcas uncertainly. "I've never seen one here. There were plenty in the store. 'Ninety-Nine Ninety-Five with Range of Attachments for Around-the-House Cleanliness,' " he added, remembering with a sigh the familiar signs.

"No, it's not a thing like that," said Grimma, "It's what you get when no one's in charge. I've been reading about them."

"*I'm* in charge, aren't I?" said Dorcas plaintively.

"No," said Grimma. "Because no one really listens to you."

"Oh. Thank you very much."

"It's not your fault. People like Masklin and Angalo and Gurder can make people listen to them, but you don't seem to keep their attention."

"Oh."

"But you can make nuts and bolts listen to you. Not everyone can do that."

Dorcas thought about this. He would never have put it like that himself. Was it a compliment? He decided it probably was.

"When people are faced with lots of troubles and they don't know what to do, there's always someone ready to say anything, just to get some power," said Grimma.

"Never mind. When the others get back I'm sure they'll sort it all out," said Dorcas, more cheerfully than he felt.

"Yes, they'll . . ." Grimma began, and then stopped. After a while Dorcas realized that her shoulders were shaking.

"Is there anything the matter?" he said.

"It's been more than three whole days!" sobbed Grimma. "No one's ever been away that long before! Something must have happened to them!"

"Er," said Dorcas. "Well, they were going to look

for Grandson Richard, 39, and we can't be sure that—"

"And I was so nasty to him before he went! I told him about the frogs and all he could think of was socks!"

Dorcas couldn't quite see how frogs had got involved. When he sat and talked to the Cat, frogs were never dragged into the conversation.

"Er?" he said.

Grimma, in between sobs, told him about the frogs.

"And I'm sure he didn't even begin to understand what I meant," she mumbled. "And you won't either."

"Oh, I don't know," said Dorcas. "You mean that the world was once so simple, and suddenly it's full of amazingly interesting things that you'll never ever get to the end of as long as you live. Like biology. Or climatology. I mean, before all you Outsiders came, I was just tinkering with things and I really didn't know anything about the world."

He stared at his feet. "I'm still very ignorant," he said, "but at least I'm ignorant about really important things. Like what the sun is, and why it rains. That's what you're talking about."

She sniffed, and smiled a bit, but not too much because if there is one thing worse than someone who doesn't understand you it's someone who understands perfectly, before you've had a chance to have a good pout about not being understood.

"The thing *is*," she said, "that he still thinks I'm

the person he used to know when we all lived in the old hole in the bank. You know, running around. Cooking things. Bandaging up people when they'd been hur-hur-hur—"

"Now then, now then," said Dorcas. He was always at a loss when people acted like this. When machines went funny you just oiled them or prodded them or, if nothing else worked, hit them with a hammer. Nomes didn't respond well to this treatment.

"Supposing he never comes back?" she said, dabbing at her eyes.

"Of course he'll come back," said Dorcas reassuringly. "What could have happened to him, after all?"

"He could have been eaten or run over or trodden on or blown away or fallen down a hole or trapped," said Grimma.

"Er, yes," said Dorcas. "Apart from that, I meant."

"But I shall pull myself together," said Grimma, sticking out her chin. "When he *does* come back, he won't be able to say, 'Oh, I see everything's gone to pieces while I've been away.' "

"Jolly good," said Dorcas. "That's the spirit. Keep yourself occupied, that's what I always say. What's the book called?"

"It's *A Treasury of Proverbs and Quotations,*" said Grimma.

"Oh. Anything useful in it?"

"That," said Grimma distantly, "depends."

"Oh. What's proverbs mean?"

"Not sure. Some of them don't make much sense. Do you know, humans think the world was made by a sort of big human?"

"No! Are you sure?"

"It took a week."

"I expect it had some help, then," said Dorcas. "You know. With the heavy stuff." Dorcas thought of the Cat. You could do a lot in a week, with the Cat helping.

"No. All by itself, apparently."

"Hmm." Dorcas considered this. Certainly bits of the world were rough, and things like grass seemed simple enough. But from what he'd heard it all broke down every year and had to be started up again in the spring, and . . . "I don't know," he said. "Only humans could believe something like that. I think you'd need more than one week. There's a good few months work, if I'm any judge."

Grimma turned the page. "Masklin used to believe—I mean, Masklin *believes*—that humans are much brighter than we think." She looked thoughtful. "I really wish we could study them properly," she said. "I'm sure we could learn a—"

For the second time, the alarm bell rang out across the quarry.

This time, the hand on the switch belonged to Nisodemus.

Seven

II. And Nisodemus said, You are betrayed,
People of the Store;

III. Falsely you were led into This Outside of
Rain and Cold and Humans and Order,
and Yet it Will become Worse;

IV. For there will be Sleet and Snow, and
Hunger in the Land;

V. And there will come Robins;

VI. Um.

VII. Yet those that brought you here, where
are they Now?

VIII. They said, We go to seek Grandson
Richard, 39, but tribulation abounds on
every side and no help comes. You are
betrayed into the hands of Winter.

IX. It is time to put aside things of the
Outside.
—From the *Book of Nome, Complaints, v. II–IX*

"Yes. Well. That's hard to do, isn't it?" said a nome
uneasily. "I mean, we *are* Outside."

"But I have a *plan,*" said Nisodemus.

"Ah," said the nomes, in unison. Plans were the thing. Plans were what was needed. You knew where you were, with a plan.

Grimma and Dorcas, almost the last to arrive, sidled their way into the crowd. The old engineer was going to push his way to the front, but Grimma restrained him.

"Look at the others up there," she whispered.

There were quite a few nomes behind Nisodemus. Many of them Dorcas recognized as Stationeri, but there were a few others from some of the great departmental families. They weren't looking at Nisodemus as he spoke, but at the crowd. Their eyes flickered back and forth, as though they were searching for something.

"I don't like the look of this," said Grimma quietly. "The big families never used to get on too well with the Stationeri, so why are they up there now?"

"Grubby pieces of work, some of them," said Dorcas.

Some of the Stationeri had been particularly upset about common, everyday nomes learning to read. They said it gave people ideas, Dorcas gathered, which were not a good thing unless they were the right kind of ideas. And some of the great families hadn't been too happy about nomes being able to go where they pleased, without having to ask permission.

They're all up there, he thought—the nomes

who haven't done so well since the Drive. They all lost a little power.

Nisodemus was explaining his plan.

As he listened, Dorcas's mouth slowly dropped open.

It was magnificent in its way, that plan. It was like a machine where every single part was perfectly made, but had been put together by a one-handed nome in the dark. It was crammed full of good ideas which you couldn't sensibly argue with, but they had been turned upside down. The trouble was, they were still ones you couldn't sensibly argue with, because the basically good idea was still in there somewhere.

Nisodemus wanted to rebuild the Store.

The nomes stood in horrified admiration as the Stationeri explained that, yes, Abbot Gurder *had* been right, when they left the Store they had taken Arnold Bros. (est. 1905) with them *inside their heads.* And, if they could show him that they really *cared* about the Store, he would come out again and put a stop to all these problems and reestablish the Store here, in this green unpleasant land.

That was how it all arrived in Dorcas's head, anyway. He'd long ago decided that if you spent all your time listening to what people actually *said* you'd never have time to work out what they *meant.*

But it wouldn't mean building the whole Store, said Nisodemus, his eyes shining like two bright black marbles. They could change the quarry in other ways. Go back to living in proper Departments instead of any old how all over the place. Put up some signs. Get back to the Good Old Ways. Make Arnold Bros. (est. 1905) feel at home. Build the Store *inside their heads.*

Nomes didn't often go mad. Dorcas vaguely recalled an elderly nome who had once decided that he was a teapot, but he'd changed his mind after a few days.

Nisodemus, though, had definitely been getting too much fresh air.

It was obvious that one or two other nomes thought so too.

"I don't quite see," said one of them, "how Arnold Bros. (est. 1905) is going to stop these humans. No offense meant."

"Did humans interfere with us when we were in the Store?" demanded Nisodemus.

"Well, no, because—"

"Then trust in Arnold Bros. (est. 1905)!"

"But that didn't keep the Store from being demolished, did it?" said a voice. "When it came to it, you all trusted Masklin and Gurder and the Truck. And yourselves! Nisodemus is always telling you how clever you are. Try and *be* clever, then!"

Dorcas realised it was Grimma. He'd never seen anyone so angry.

She pushed her way through the apprehensive nomes until she was face to face or at least, since he was standing on something and she wasn't, face to chest. Nisodemus was one of those people who liked standing on things.

"What will actually *happen*, then?" she shouted. "When you've built the Store, what will *happen*? Humans came into the Store, you know!"

Nisodemus's mouth opened and shut for a while. Then he said, "But they obeyed the regulations! Yes! Um! That's what they did! And things were better then!"

She glared at him.

"You don't really think people are going to accept that, do you?" she said.

There was silence.

"You've got to admit," said an elderly nome, very slowly, "things *were* better then."

The nomes shuffled their feet.

That was all you could hear.

Just people, shuffling their feet.

"They just accepted it!" said Grimma, "Just like that! No one's bothered about the council anymore! They just do what he tells them! Even Granny Morkie's no help! She just sits around with all the old people, talking! I told her she should help me, and all she said was that she's too old to worry about young fools like Nisodemus! She says, in ten years' time who'll care?"

Now she was in Dorcas's workspace under a bench in the old quarry garage. My little sanctuary, he always called it. My little nook. Bits of wire and tin were scattered everywhere. The wall was covered with scrawls done with a bit of pencil lead.

Dorcas sat and twirled a bit of wire aimlessly.

"You're being hard on people," he said quietly. "You shouldn't yell at them like that. They've been through a lot. They get all confused if you shout at them. The council was all right for when times were good . . ." He shrugged. "And without Masklin and Gurder and Angalo, well, it hardly seems worthwhile."

"But after all that's happened!" She waved her arms. "To act so *stupidly,* just because he's offered them—"

"A bit of comfort," said Dorcas. He shook his head. You couldn't explain things like this to people like Grimma. Nice girl, bright head on her, but she kept thinking that everyone else was as passionate about things as she was. All people *really* wanted, Dorcas considered, was to be left alone. The world was quite difficult enough as it was without people going around trying to make it better all the time.

Masklin had understood that. He knew the way to make people do what you wanted was to make them think it was their idea. If there was one thing that got right up a nome's nose, it was people saying to them, "Here is a really sensible idea—what are you, too *stupid* to understand?"

It wasn't that people *were* stupid. It was just that people were people.

"Come on," he said wearily. "Let's go and see how the signs are getting on."

The whole of the floor of one of the big sheds had been turned over to the making of the signs. Or rather, the Signs. Another thing Nisodemus was good at was giving words capital letters. You could *hear* him doing it.

Dorcas had to admit that the Signs were a pretty good idea, though. He felt guilty about thinking this.

He'd thought that when Nisodemus had summoned him and asked if there was any paint in the quarry, only now the quarry was being called the New Store.

"Um," Dorcas had said, "There are some old paint cans, white and red, mainly, under one of the benches. We might be able to lever the tops off."

"Then do it. It is very important. Um. We must make Signs," said the Stationeri.

"Signs. Right," said Dorcas. "Cheer the place up a bit, you mean?"

"No!"

"Sorry, sorry, I just thought—"

"Signs for the gate!"

Dorcas scratched his chin. "The gate?" he said.

"Humans obey Signs," said Nisodemus, calming down. "We know that. Did they not obey the Signs in the Store?"

"Most of 'em," agreed Dorcas. "Dogs and Strollers Must Be Carried" had always puzzled him. Lots of humans didn't carry either.

"Signs make humans do things," said Nisodemus, "Or stop doing things. So get to work, good Dorcas. Signs. Um. *Signs that say 'No.'* "

Dorcas had given this a lot of thought as teams of nomes sweated to pry open the lids of the paint-streaked cans. They still had the High Way Code from the Truck, and there were plenty of signs in there. And he could remember some of the signs from the Store.

Then there was a stroke of luck. Normally the nomes stayed at floor level, but Dorcas had taken to sending his young assistants onto the big desk in the quarry manager's office occasionally, where there were useful scraps of paper. Now he needed to work out what the signs should say.

Sacco and Nooty came back with the news.

They'd found more signs. Old ones. A great big grubby notice pinned to the wall, covered with signs.

"Masses of them," Sacco said, coming back out of breath. "And you know what, sir? You know what? I read what it said on the notice and it said, 'Health and Safety at Work,' it said, 'Obey These Signs,' it said, and it said, 'They Are There for Your Protection.' "

"That's what it said?" said Dorcas.

" 'For Your Protection,' " Sacco repeated.

"Can you get it down?"

"There's a coathook next to it," said Nooty enthusiastically. "I bet we could sling a hook up and then pull it over toward the window, and then—"

"Yes, yes, you're good at that sort of thing," said Dorcas. Nooty could climb like a squirrel. "I expect Nisodemus will be very pleased," he added.

Nisodemus was, especially with the piece that said "For Your Protection." It showed, he said, that, um, Arnold Bros. (est. 1905) was on their side.

Every bit of board and rusty sheet of metal had to be pressed into service. The nomes went at it cheerfully enough, though, happy to be doing something. Next morning the sun rose to see a variety of Signs hanging, not always squarely, on the battered quarry gate.

They had been very thorough. The Signs said: NO ETNRY. EXIT THIS WAY. DAGNER—HARD HAT AREA. BLASTIGN IN PROGRES. ALL TRUCKS REPORT TO WIEGH-IN STATION. SLIPERY WHEN WET. THIS REGESTIR CLOSED. ELEVOTAR OUT FO ORDER. BEWARE OF FLALING ROCKS. ROAD FLOOODED.

And one that Dorcas had found in a book and was rather proud of: UNEXPLODED BOM.

Just to be on the safe side, though, and without telling Nisodemus, he found some more chain and, in one of the greasy old toolboxes in the Cat's shed, a padlock nearly as big as he was. It took four nomes to carry it.

The chain was massive. Some of the nomes found Dorcas painstakingly levering it along across the quarry floor, one link at a time. He didn't seem to want to tell them where he'd found it.

* * *

The truck turned up around noon. The nomes, waiting in the hedge by the side of the truck, saw the driver get out, look at the signs, and . . .

No, that wasn't right. Humans couldn't do that sort of thing. It couldn't be true. But twenty nomes, peering out from the undergrowth, saw it happen.

The human disobeyed the signs.

Not only that, it pulled some of them off the gate and threw them away.

They watched in astonishment. Even UNEX-PLODED BOM was whirled into the bushes, nearly knocking young Sacco from his perch.

The new chain, though, caused the human a few problems. It rattled the chain once or twice, peered in through the wire mesh of the gate, stamped around for a bit, and then drove off.

The nomes in the bushes cheered, but not too happily.

If humans weren't going to do what was expected of them, nothing was right in the world.

"I reckon that's it," said Dorcas when they got back. "I don't like the idea any more than anyone else, but we've got to move. I know humans. That chain won't stop them if they really want to get in."

"I absolutely forbid anyone to leave!" said Nisodemus.

"But you see, metal can be cut through—" Dorcas began in a reasonable tone of voice.

"Silence!" shouted Nisodemus. "It's your fault, you old fool! Um! You put the chain on the gate!"

"Well, you see, it was to stop the—pardon?" said Dorcas.

"If you *hadn't* put the chain on the gate, the signs *would* have stopped the human," said Nisodemus. "But you can't expect Arnold Bros. (est. 1905) to help us if we show we don't trust him!"

"Um," said Dorcas. What he was thinking was: Mad. A mad nome. A dangerously mad nome. We're not talking about teapots here. He backed out of Nisodemus's presence and was glad to get out into the bitingly cold air.

Everything's going wrong, he thought. I was left in charge, and now it's all going wrong, we haven't got any proper plans, Masklin hasn't come back, and it's all going wrong.

If humans come into the quarry, they'll find us.

Something cold landed on his head. He brushed at it irritably.

I'll have a word with some of the younger nomes, he thought. Maybe going to the barn wasn't such a bad idea. We could keep our eyes shut on the way. Or something.

Something else, cold and soft, settled on his neck.

Oh, why are people so *complicated?*

He looked up and realized that he couldn't see the other side of the quarry. The air was full of white specks, and more appeared as he watched.

He watched it in horror.

It was snowing.

Eight

VII. And Grimma said, We have two choices.
VIII. We can run, or we can hide.
 IX. And they said, Which shall we do?
  X. She said, We shall Fight.
—From the *Book of Nome, Quarries III, v. VII–X*

It wasn't much of a snowfall, just one of those nippy little sprinklings that come early in the winter to make it absolutely clear that it is, well, the winter. That's what Granny Morkie said.

She'd never been very interested in the council anyway. She liked to spend her time with the other old people, exchanging grumbles and, as she put it, cheerin' them up and takin' them out o' themselves.

She strutted around in the snow as if it belonged to her.

The old-Store nomes watched her in horrified silence.

" 'Course, this is nothing to some of 'em," she said. "I mind we've had snow so deep we couldn't

· *78* ·

walk around in it, we had to dig tunnels! Talk about laugh!"

"Er, madam," said a very old nome, gravely, "Does it always drop out of the sky like this?"

" 'Course! Sometimes it gets blown along by the wind. You get great big piles!"

"We thought it—you see, on the cards—that is, in the Store—well, we thought it just sort of appeared on things," said the old nome. "In a rather jolly and festive way," he added, looking embarrassed.

They watched it pile up. Over the quarry the clouds hung like overstuffed mattresses.

"At least it means we won't have to go to that horrid barn place," said a nome.

"That's right," said Granny Morkie. "You could catch your death, going out in this." She looked cheerful.

The old nomes grumbled among themselves, and scanned the sky anxiously for the first signs of robins or reindeer.

The snow closed the quarry in. You couldn't see out across the fields.

Dorcas sat in his workshop and stared at the snow piling up against the dirty window, giving the shed a dull gray light.

"Well," he said quietly, "we wanted to be shut away. And now we are. We can't run away, and we can't hide. We ought to have gone when Masklin left."

He heard footsteps behind him. It was Grimma.

She spent a long time near the gate these days, but the snow had driven her indoors at last.

"He wouldn't be able to come," she said. "Not in the snow."

"Yeah. Right," said Dorcas uncertainly.

"It's been eight days now."

"Yes. Quite a long time."

"What were you saying when I came in?" she said.

"I was just talking to myself. Does this snow stuff stay for a long time?"

"Granny says it does, sometimes. Weeks and weeks, she says."

"Oh."

"When the humans come back, they'll be here for good," said Grimma.

"Yes," said Dorcas sadly. "Yes, I think you're right."

"How many of us would be able to . . . you know . . . go on living here?"

"A couple of dozen, perhaps. If they don't eat much, and lie low during the day. There's no Food Hall, you see." He sighed. "And there won't be much hunting. Not with humans around the quarry the whole time. All the game up in the thickets will run away."

"But there's thousands of us!"

Dorcas shrugged.

"It's hard enough for me to walk through this snow," he said. "There's hundreds of older nomes who'll never do it. And young ones, come to that."

"So we've got to stay, just as Nisodemus wants," said Grimma.

"Yes. Stay and hope. Perhaps the snow will be gone. We could make a run for the thickets or something," he said vaguely.

"We could stay and fight," said Grimma.

Dorcas growled. "Oh, that's easy. We fight all the time. Bicker, bicker, bicker. That's nomish nature for you."

"I mean, fight the humans. Fight for the quarry."

There was a long pause.

Then Dorcas said, "What, us? Fight *humans?*"

"Yes."

"But they're *humans!*"

"Yes."

"But they're so much bigger than we are!" said Dorcas desperately.

"Then they'll make better targets," said Grimma, her eyes alight. "And we're faster than them, and smarter than them, and we know they exist and we have," she added, "the element of surprise."

"The what?" said Dorcas, totally lost.

"The element of surprise. They don't know we're here," she explained.

He gave her a sidelong glance.

"You've been reading strange books again," he said.

"Well, it's better than sitting around wringing our hands and saying, 'Oh dear, oh dear, the humans are coming and we shall all be squashed.'"

"That's all very well," said Dorcas. "But what are you suggesting? Bashing them over the head would be really tricky, take it from me."

"Not their heads," said Grimma.

Dorcas stared at her. Fight humans? It was such a novel idea it was hard to get your mind around it.

But . . . well, there was that book, wasn't there? The one Masklin had found in the Store, the one that had given him the idea for driving the truck. What was it? *Gulliver's Travels*? And there'd been this picture of a human lying down, with what looked like nomes tying it up with hundreds of ropes. Not even the oldest nomes could remember it ever happening; it must have been a long time ago.

A snag struck him.

"Hang on a minute," he said. "If we start fighting humans . . ." His voice trailed off.

"Yes?" said Grimma impatiently.

"They'll start fighting us, won't they? I know they're not very bright, but it'll dawn on them that something's happening and they'll fight back. Retaliation, that's called."

"That's right," said Grimma. "And that's why it's vitally important we retaliate right at the start."

Dorcas thought about this. It seemed a logical idea.

"But only in self-defense," he said. "Only in self-defense. Even with humans. I don't want there to be any unnecessary suffering."

"I suppose so," she said.

"You really think we could fight humans?"

"Oh, yes."

"So . . . how?"

Grimma bit her lip. "Hmm," she said, "Young Sacco and his friends. Can you trust them?"

"They're keen lads. And lasses, one or two of them." He smiled. "Always ready for something new."

"Right. Then we shall need some nails . . ."

"You've really been thinking hard, haven't you?" said Dorcas. He was almost in awe. Grimma was often bad tempered. He thought perhaps it was because her mind worked very fast, sometimes, and she was impatient with people who weren't keeping up. But now she was furious. You could begin to feel sorry for any humans who got in her way.

"I've been doing a lot of reading," she said.

"Er, yes. Yes, I can see," said Dorcas. "But, er, I wonder if it wouldn't be more sensible to—"

"We're not going to run away again," she said flatly. "We shall fight them on the tracks. We shall fight them at the gates. We shall fight them in the quarry. And we shall never surrender."

"What does 'surrender' mean?" said Dorcas, desperately.

"We don't know the meaning of surrender," said Grimma.

"Well, *I* don't," said Dorcas.

Grimma leaned against the wall.

"Do you want to hear something strange?" she said.

Dorcas thought about it.

"I don't mind," he said.

"There's books about us."

"Like Gulliver, you mean?"

"No. That was about a human. About us, I mean. Ordinary-size people, like us. But wearing all green suits and with little knobbly stalks on their heads. Sometimes humans put out bowls of milk for us and we do all the housework for them. And we have wings, like bees. That's what gets put in books about us. They call us pixies. It's in a book called *Fairy Tales for Little Folk.*"

"I don't think the wings would work," said Dorcas doubtfully. "I don't think you could get the lifting power."

"And they think we live in mushrooms," Grimma finished.

"Hmm? Doesn't sound very practical to me," said Dorcas.

"And they think we repair shoes."

"That's a bit more like it," said Dorcas. "Good solid work."

"And the book said we paint the flowers to make them pretty colors," said Grimma.

Dorcas thought about this.

"Nah," he said eventually. "I've looked at the colors on flowers. They're definitely built-in."

"We're real," said Grimma. "We do real things. So why do you think that sort of thing goes in books?"

"Search me," said Dorcas. "I only read manuals.

It's not a proper book, I've always said, unless it's got lists and line drawings in it."

"If ever humans do catch us, that's what we'll become," said Grimma. "Sweet little people, painting flowers. They won't let us be anything else. They'll turn us into *little* people." She sighed. "Do you ever get the feeling you'll never know anything you ought to know?"

"Oh, yes. All the time."

Grimma frowned.

"*I* know one thing," she said. "When Masklin comes back, he's going to have somewhere to come back to."

"Oh," said Dorcas.

"Oh," he repeated. "Oh. I see."

It was bitterly cold in the Cat's lair. Other nomes never came in, because it was drafty and stank. That suited Dorcas fine.

He padded across the floor and went under the huge tarpaulin where the Cat lived. It took quite a long time to climb up to his preferred perch on the monster, even using the bits of wood and string he'd painstakingly tied to him . . . *it.*

He sat down and waited until he got his breath back.

"I only want to help people," he said quietly. "Like giving them things like electricity and making their lives better. But they never say thank you, you know. They wanted me to paint signs, so I painted signs. Now Grimma wants to fight humans. She's got lots of ideas out of books. I know she's doing it to help forget about Masklin but no good will come of it, you mark my words. But if I don't help, things will only get worse. I don't want *anybody* to get hurt. People like us can't be repaired as easily as people like you."

He drummed his heels on the Cat's—what would it be?—the Cat's neck, probably.

"It's all right for you," he said. "Sleeping quietly here all the time. Having a nice rest . . ."

He stared at the Cat for a long while.

Then, very quietly, he said, "I wonder . . . ?"

Five long minutes went past. Dorcas appeared and reappeared among the complicated shadows, muttering to himself, saying things like, "That's dead, that's no good, we need a new battery," and "Seems okay, nothing that a good clean couldn't put right," and "Hmm, not much in your tank . . ."

Finally he walked out from under the dusty tarp and rubbed his hands together.

Everyone has a purpose in life, he thought. It's what keeps them going.

Nisodemus wants things to be as they were. Grimma wants Masklin back. And Masklin . . . no one knows exactly what it is that Masklin wants, except that it's very big.

But they all have this *purpose*. If you have a purpose in life, you can feel six inches tall.

And now I've found one.

Wow.

* * *

The human came back later and it did not come alone. There was the Land-Rover and a much larger truck, with the words Blackbury Stone and Gravel Inc. painted on the side. Its tires turned the thin coating of snow into glistening mud.

It jolted up the dirt road, slowed down as it came out into the open area in front of the quarry gates, and stopped.

It wasn't a very good stop. The back of the vehicle swung around and nearly hit the hedge. The engine coughed into silence.

There was the sound of hissing. And, very slowly, the truck sank.

Two humans got out. They walked around the truck, looking at each tire in turn.

"They're only flat at the bottom," whispered Grimma, in their hiding place in the bushes.

"Don't worry about it," hissed Dorcas. "The thing about tires is, the flat bit always sinks to the bottom. Amazing what you can do with a few nails, isn't it?"

The smaller truck stopped behind the first one. Two humans got out of that, too, and joined the others. One of them was holding the longest pair of pliers Dorcas had ever seen. While the rest of the humans bent down by one of the flat tires it strolled up to the gate, fiddled the teeth of the pliers onto the padlock, and squeezed.

It was an effort, even for a human. But there was a snap loud enough to be heard even in the bushes, and then a long drawn-out clinking noise as the chain fell away.

Dorcas groaned. He'd had great hopes for that chain. It was the Cat's; at least, it was in a big yellow box bolted to part of the Cat, so presumably it had belonged to the Cat. But it had been the padlock that had broken, not the chain. Dorcas felt oddly proud about that.

"I don't understand it," Grimma muttered. "They can see they're not wanted, so why are they so stupid?"

"It's not as if there aren't masses of stone around," agreed Sacco.

The human pulled at the gate and swung it enough to allow itself inside.

"It's going to the manager's office," said Sacco. "It's going to make noises in the telephone."

"No, it's not," Dorcas prophesied.

"But it will be ringing up Order," said Sacco. "It'll be saying, in Human, I mean, it'll be saying, Some of Our Wheels Have Gone Flat."

"No," said Dorcas, "It'll be saying, Why Doesn't the Telephone Work?"

"Why doesn't the telephone work?" said Nooty.

"Because I know which wires to cut," said Dorcas. "Look, it's coming back out."

They watched it walk around the sheds. The snow had covered the nomes' sad attempts at cultivation. There were plenty of nome tracks, though, like little bird trails in the snow. The human didn't

notice them. Humans hardly ever noticed anything.

"Trip wires," said Grimma.

"What?" said Dorcas.

"Trip wires. We should put trip wires down.
The bigger they are," said Grimma, "the harder
they fall."

"Not on us, I hope," said Dorcas.

"No. We could put more nails down," said
Grimma.

"Good grief."

The humans clustered around the stricken truck.
Then they appeared to reach a decision and walked
back to the Land-Rover. They got in. It couldn't go
forward, but reversed slowly down the dirt road,
turned around in a field gateway, and headed back
to the main road. The big truck was left alone.

Dorcas breathed out.

"I was afraid one of them would stay," he said.

"They'll come back," said Grimma. "You've always said it. Humans'll come back and mend the
wheels or whatever it is they do."

"Then we'd better get on with it," said Dorcas.
"Come on, everybody."

He stood up and trotted toward the road. To Sacco's surprise, Dorcas was whistling under his
breath.

"Now, the important thing is to make sure they
can't move it," he said as they ran to keep up. "If
they can't move it, it means it stays blocking the

dirt road. And if it stays blocking the dirt road, they can't get any more machines in."

"Good thinking," said Grimma, in a slightly puzzled voice.

"We must immobilize it," said Dorcas. "We'll take out the battery first. No electricity, no go."

"Right," said Sacco.

"It's a big square thing," said Sacco, "It'll need eight of you at least. Don't drop it, whatever you do."

"Why not?" said Grimma. "We want to smash it, don't we?"

"Er. Er. Er," said Dorcas urgently, like a motor trying to get started. "No, because, because it could be dangerous. Yes. Dangerous. Yes. Because, because, because of the acid and whatnot. You must take it out very carefully, and I'll find somewhere safe to put it. Yes. Very safe. Off you go now. Two men to a wrench."

They trotted off.

"What else can we do?" said Grimma.

"We'd better drain the gas out," said Dorcas firmly as they walked under the shadow of the truck. It was much smaller than the one that had brought them out of the Store, but still quite big enough. He wandered around until he was under the enormous swelling bulk of the gas tank.

Four of the young nomes had dragged an empty can out of the bushes. Dorcas called them over and pointed to the tank above them.

"There must be a nut on there somewhere," he

said. "It'll be to let the stuff out. Get a wrench around it. Make sure the can's underneath it first!"

They nodded enthusiastically and got to work. Nomes are good climbers and remarkably strong for their size.

"And try not to spill any, please!" Dorcas shouted up after them.

"I don't see why that matters," said Grimma, behind him. "All we want to do is get it out of the truck. Where it *goes* doesn't matter, does it?"

She gave him another thoughtful look. Dorcas blinked back at her, his mind racing.

"Ah," he said. "Ah. Ah. Because. Becausebecausebecause. Ah. Because it's dangerous stuff. We don't want it polluting things, do we? Best to put it carefully in a can and—"

"Keep it safe?" said Grimma suspiciously.

"Right! Right," said Dorcas, who was starting to sweat. "Good idea. Now let's just go over here . . ." He led Grimma away.

There was sudden rush of air and a thump from right behind them. The truck's battery landed where they had been standing.

"Sorry, Dorcas," Sacco called down. "It was a lot heavier than we thought. It got away from us."

"You idiots!" Grimma shouted.

"Yes, you idiots!" shouted Dorcas. "You might have damaged it! Just you come down here right now and get it into the hedge, quickly!"

"He might have damaged *us*!" said Grimma.

"Yes. Yes. Yes, that's what I meant, of course,"

said Dorcas vaguely. "You wouldn't mind organizing them a bit, would you? They're good boys, but always a little too enthusiastic, if you know what I mean."

He wandered off into the shadow, his head tilted backward.

"Well!" said Grimma. She looked around at Sacco and his friends, who were sheepishly climbing down again.

"Don't just stand there," she said. "Get it into the hedge. Hasn't Dorcas told you about using levers? Very important things. It's amazing what you can do with levers. We used them a lot on the Long Drive . . ."

Her voice trailed off. She turned and looked at the distant figure of Dorcas and her eyes narrowed.

The cunning old devil is up to something, she thought.

"Oh, just get on with it," she said, and ran after Dorcas.

He was standing under the truck's engine, staring up intently into the masses of rusting pipework. As she came up she distinctly heard him say, "Now, what else do we need?"

"What do you mean, need?" said Grimma quietly.

"Oh, to help the Ca—" Dorcas stopped, and turned around slowly. "I mean, what else do we need to *do* to make the thing totally immobile," he said stonily. "That was what I meant."

"You're not planning to drive this truck, are you?" said Grimma.

"Don't be silly. Where'd we go? It'd never get across the fields to the barn."

"Well. All right, then."

"I just want to have a look around it. Time spent collecting knowledge is never wasted," said Dorcas primly. He stepped out into the light on the other side of the truck and looked up.

"Well, well," he said.

"What is it?"

"They left the door open. I suppose they thought it was all right because they'd be coming back."

Grimma followed his gaze. The truck's door *was* slightly ajar.

Dorcas looked around at the hedge behind them.

"Help me find a big enough stick," he said. "I reckon we could climb up there and have a look around."

"A look around? What do you expect to find?"

"You never know till you've looked," said Dorcas philosophically. He peered back underneath the truck.

"How are you all doing under there? We need a hand here."

Sacco staggered up. "We managed to get the battery thing behind the hedge," he said, "and the can's nearly full. Smells horrible. There's still lots coming out."

"Can you get the screw back in?"

"Nooty tried and she got all covered in yuk."

"Let it go on the road, then," said Dorcas.

"Hang on, you said that would be dangerous," said Grimma. "It's dangerous until you've filled the can up, is it, and then not dangerous at all?"

"Look, you wanted me to stop the truck and I've stopped the truck," said Dorcas. "So just shut up, will you?"

Grimma looked at him in horror.

"What did you say?" she said.

Dorcas swallowed. Oh, well. If you were going to get shouted at, you might as well get your money's worth.

"I said just shut up," he said quietly. "I don't want to be rude, but you do go on at people. I'm sorry, but that's how it is. I'm helping you. I'm not asking you to help me, but at least you can let me get on with things instead of badgering me the whole time. And you never say please or thank you, either. People are a little like machines," he added solemnly, while her face went redder, "and words like please and thank you are just like grease. They make them work better. Is that all right?" He turned to the boys, who were looking embarrassed.

"Find a stick long enough to reach up to the cab," he said. "Please."

They fell over themselves to obey.

Nine

III. The younger nomes spoke, *saying,* Would
that we were the nomes our fathers were,
to ride upon the Truck, and what was it
like.
IV. And Dorcas said, It was scary.
V. That was what it was like.
—From the *Book of Nome, Strange Frogs II, v. III–V*

It was pretty much like the cab of the truck that
had brought them from the Store. It brought back
old memories.

"Wow!" said Sacco, "And we all drove one of
these?"

"Seven hundred of us," said Dorcas proudly.
"Your dad was one of them. You were in the back
with your mothers. All you lads were."

"I'm not a lad," said Nooty.

"Sorry," said Dorcas. "Slip of the tongue. In my
day girls stayed at home most of the time. Not that
I've got anything at all against them getting out
and about a bit now," he added hurriedly, not

wanting another Grimma on his hands. "I'm not against that at all."

"I wish I'd been older on the Drive," said Nooty. "It must have been *amazing.*"

"It terrified the life out of me," said Dorcas.

The others wandered around the cab like tourists in a cathedral, gawking. Nooty tried to press a pedal.

"Amazing," she said, under her breath.

"Sacco, you get up there and take those keys out," said Dorcas. "The rest of you, no lollygagging. Those humans could be back anytime. Nooty, stop making those brrrm-brrrm noises. I'm sure nice girls shouldn't make those kind of noises," he added lamely.

Sacco swarmed up the steering wheel post and wrestled the keys out of the ignition while the rest of the boys poked around in the cab.

Grimma wasn't with them. She hadn't wanted to come up into the cab. She'd gone very quiet, in fact. She'd stayed down in the dirt road with a sullen look on her face.

But it had needed saying, Dorcas told himself.

He looked around the cab. Let's see, he thought . . . we've got the battery, we've got the fuel, was there anything else the Cat needs?

"Come on, everyone," he called, "Let's be getting out of here. Nooty, stop trying to *move* things all the time. It'd take all of you to shift the gear lever. Come on, before the humans come back."

He made his way to the door and heard a click behind him.

"I said come on— *What do you think you're doing?*"

The young nomes stared at him, wide-eyed.

"We're seeing if we can move the gear lever, Dorcas," said Nooty, "If you press this knob you can—"

"Don't press the knob! Don't press the knob!"

The first inkling Grimma had that something was going wrong was a nasty little crunching sound and a change in the light.

The truck was moving. Not very fast, because the two front tires were flat. But the dirt road was steep. It was moving all right, and just because it had started off slowly didn't mean there wasn't something huge and unstoppable about it.

She stared at it in horror.

The dirt road ran between high banks all the way down to the big highway—and the railroad.

"I said don't press it! Did I say press it? I said don't press it!"

The terrified nomes stared it him, their open mouths a row of Os.

"It's not the gear lever! It's the hand brake, you idiots!"

Now they could all hear the crunching noise and feel the slight vibration.

"Er," said Sacco, his voice shaking, "What's a hand brake, Dorcas?"

"It keeps it stopped on hills and things! Don't just stand there! Help me push it back up!"

The cab was, very gently, beginning to sway from side to side. The truck was definitely moving. The hand brake wasn't. Dorcas heaved on it until blue and purple spots flashed in front of his eyes.

"I just gave the knob on the end a push!" Nooty babbled. "I only wanted to see what it did!"

"Yes, yes, all right . . ." Dorcas stared around. What he needed was a lever. What he needed was about fifty nomes. What he needed most of all was not to be here.

He staggered across the bouncing floor to the doorway and cautiously peered out. The hedge was moving past quite gently, as if it wasn't in a particular hurry to get anywhere, but the surface of the road already had a blurred look.

We could probably jump, he thought. And if we're lucky, we won't break anything. If we're even luckier, we'll avoid the wheels. How lucky do I feel, right at this minute?

Not very.

Sacco joined him.

"Perhaps if we took a good running jump—" he began.

There was a thump as the truck hit the bank, heeled over, and then bounced back onto the road.

The nomes struggled to their feet.

"On the other hand, perhaps not a good idea," said Sacco. "What shall we do now, Dorcas?"

"Just hang on," said Dorcas. "I think the banks

will keep it on the road and I suppose it'll just roll to a halt eventually." He sat down suddenly as the truck bounced off the bank again. "You wanted to know what a truck ride was like. Well, now you know."

There was another thump. The branch of a tree caught the door, swung it open and then, with a terrible metallic noise, ripped it off.

"Was it like this?" shouted Nooty, above the noise. To Dorcas's amazement, now that the immediate danger was over, she seemed to be quite enjoying it. We're bringing up new nomes, he thought. They're not so scared of things as we were. They know about a bigger world.

He coughed.

"Well, apart from its being in the dark and we could see where we were going, yes," he said. "I think we all ought to hang on to something. Just in case it gets bumpy."

The truck rolled down the dirt road and onto the highway. A car skidded into the hedge to avoid it; another truck managed to stop at the end of four long streaks of scorched rubber.

None of the nomes in the cab noticed this at the time. All they felt was another thump as the truck bounced gently over the far side of the highway and down the dirt road that ran toward the railroad.

Where, with red lights flashing, the barriers were coming down.

* * *

Sacco peered out of the stricken doorway.

"We've just crossed over a paved road," he said.

"Ah," said Dorcas.

"I just saw a car run into the back of another car and a truck ended up going sideways," Sacco went on.

"Ah. Lucky we got over, then," said Dorcas. "There's some dangerous drivers around."

The gritty sound of the flat tires rolling over gravel gradually slowed down. There was the snap of something breaking behind the truck, a couple of bumps, and then another thump that brought them to a halt.

And a low, booming noise.

Nomes hear things differently from humans, and the shrill clanging of the crossing warning alarms sounded, to them, like the doleful tolling of an ancient bell.

"We've stopped," said Dorcas. He thought, We could have pressed the brake pedal. We could have looked for something to press it with and pressed it. I must be getting too old. Oh, well. "Come on, no hanging around. We can jump out. You youngsters can, anyway."

"Why? What are you going to do?" said Sacco.

"I'm going to wait until you've all jumped out, and then I'm going to tell you to catch me," said Dorcas pleasantly. "I'm not as young as I was. Now, off you go."

They got down awkwardly, hanging on to the

edge of the running board and dropping onto the road.

Dorcas lowered himself gingerly onto the running board and sat with his legs dangling over the drop.

It looked a long way down.

Below him, Nooty prodded Sacco respectfully on the arm.

"Er. Sacco," she said, nervously.

"What is it?"

"Look at that metal rail thing over there."

"Well, what about it?"

"There's another one over *there*, " said Nooty, pointing.

"Yes, I can see," said Sacco testily. "What about them? They're not doing anything."

"We're right in between them," said Nooty. "I just thought I should, you know, point it out. And there's that bell thing ringing."

"Yes, I can hear it," said Sacco irritably. "I wish it would stop."

"I just wondered why it was."

Sacco shrugged. "Who knows why anything happens?" he said. "Come *on*, Dorcas. *Please*. We haven't got all day."

"I'm just composing myself," said Dorcas quietly.

Nooty wandered miserably away from the group and looked down at one of the rails. It was bright and shiny.

And it seemed to be singing.

She bent closer. Yes, it was definitely making a faint humming sound. Which was odd. Bits of metal didn't normally make any noise at all. Not by themselves, anyway.

As she stared at the truck stuck between the flashing lights and the shiny rails, the world seem to change slightly and a horrible idea formed in her head.

"Sacco!" she quavered. "Sacco, we're right on the railroad line, Sacco!"

Something a long way off made a deep, mournful noise.

Whoo-oooo . . .

From the gateway of the quarry Grimma had a good view of the land all the way to the airport. She saw the train, and the truck.

The train had seen the truck too. It suddenly started to make the long drawn-out screaming noise of metal in distress.

By the time it actually *hit* the thing, it seemed to be going quite slowly. It even managed to stay on the rails.

Pieces of truck spun away in every direction, like fireworks.

Ten

I.   Nisodemus said unto them, Do you doubt
that I can stop the power of Order?
II.   And they said, Um . . .
          —From the *Book of Nome, Chases I, v. I–II*

Other nomes came running across the quarry floor,
with Nisodemus in the lead, and piled up in a
crowd around the gate.

"What happened? What happened?"

"I saw everything," said a middle-aged nome, "I
was on watch, and I saw Dorcas and some of the
boys go into the truck. And then it rolled away
down the hill and then it went over the highway
and then it stopped right on the railroad tracks and
then . . . and then . . ."

"I forbade all meddling with these infernal machines," said Nisodemus. "And I said we were to
stop, um, putting people on watch, didn't I? The
watch Arnold Bros. (est. 1905) maintains should be
enough for humble nomes!"

"Yes . . . well . . . Dorcas said he thought it

wouldn't do any harm if we gave him a hand, sort of thing," said the nome nervously. "And he said—"

"I gave *orders*!" screamed Nisodemus. "You will all obey me! Did I not stop the truck by the power of Arnold Bros. (est. 1905)?"

"No," said Grimma quietly. "No, you didn't. Dorcas did. He put nails down in the road."

There was a huge, horrified silence. In the middle of it Nisodemus went slowly white with rage.

"Liar!" he shouted.

"No," said Grimma, meekly. "He really did. He really did all sorts of things to help us, and we never said 'please' or 'thank you' and now he's dead."

There were sirens along the road below and a lot of excitement around the stationary train. Red and blue lights flashed.

The nomes shifted uneasily. One of them said, "He's not really dead, though, is he? Not *really*. I expect he jumped out at the last minute. A clever person like him."

Grimma looked helplessly at the crowd. She saw Nooty's parents in the crowd. They were a quiet, patient couple. She'd hardly ever spoken to them. Now their faces were gray and lined with worry. She gave in.

"Yes," she said. "Perhaps they got out."

"Must have," muttered another nome, trying to look cheerful. "Dorcas isn't the type to go around dying all the time. Not when we need him."

Grimma nodded.

"And now," she went on, "I think even humans will be wondering what's happening here. They'll soon work out where the truck came from and they'll be coming up here and I think they might be very angry."

But Nisodemus licked his lips and said, "We won't be afraid. We will confront them and defy them. Um. We will treat them with scorn. We don't need Dorcas, we need nothing except faith in Arnold Bros. (est. 1905). Nails, indeed!"

"If you start out now," said Grimma, "you should all be able to get to the barn, even through what's left of the snow. I don't think the quarry will be a safe place soon."

There was something about the way she said it that made people nervous. Normally Grimma shouted or argued, but this time she spoke quite calmly. It wasn't like her at all.

"Go on," she said. "You'll have to start now. You'll have to take as much food and stuff as possible. Go on."

"No!" shouted Nisodemus. "No one is to move! Do you think Arnold Bros. (est. 1905) will let you down? Um, I will protect you from the humans!"

Down below, a car with flashing lights on top of it pulled away from the excitement around the train, crossed the main highway, and headed slowly up the dirt road.

"I will call upon the power of Arnold Bros. (est. 1905) to *smite* the humans!" shouted Nisodemus.

The nomes looked unhappy. Arnold Bros. (est. 1905) had never smitten anyone in the Store. He'd just founded it, and seen to it that nomes lived comfortable and not very strenuous lives in it, and apart from putting the signs on the walls hadn't really interfered very much. Now, suddenly, he was going around being angry and upset all the time, and smiting people. It was very bewildering.

"I will stand here and defy the dreadful minions of Order!" Nisodemus yelled. "I will teach them a lesson they won't forget."

The rest of the nomes said nothing. If Nisodemus wanted to stand in front of the truck, then that was all right by them.

"We will *all* defy them!" he added.

"Er . . . what?" said a nome.

"Brothers, let us stand here resolute and show Order that we are united in opposition! Um. If you truly believe in Arnold Bros. (est. 1905), no harm will come to you!"

The flashing light was well up the road now. Soon it would be crossing the wide patch in front of the gates, where the great chain hung uselessly from the broken padlock.

Grimma opened her mouth to say: Don't be stupid, you idiots. Arnold Bros. (est. 1905) doesn't want you to stand in front of cars. I've *seen* what happens to nomes who stand in front of cars. Your relatives have to bury you in an envelope.

She was about to say all that, and decided not to.

For months and months people had been telling nomes what to do. Perhaps it was time to stop.

She saw a number of worried faces in the crowd turn toward her, and someone said, "What shall we *do*, Grimma?"

"Yeah," said another nome, "She's a Driver, they always know what to do."

She smiled at them. It wasn't a very happy smile.

"Do whatever you think best," she said.

There was a chorus of indrawn breaths.

"Well, yeah," said a nome, "but, well, Nisodemus says we can stop this thing just by believing we can. Is that true, or what?"

"I don't know," said Grimma. "You might be able to. I know I can't."

She turned and walked off quickly toward the sheds.

"Stand firm," commanded Nisodemus. He hadn't been listening to the worried discussions behind him.

" 'Do whatever you think best,' " muttered a nome. "What sort of help is that?"

They stood in their hundreds, watching the car wind closer. Nisodemus stood slightly ahead of the crowd, holding his hands in the air.

The only sound was the crunch of tires on gravel.

If a bird looked down on the quarry in the next few seconds, it would have been amazed.

Well, probably it wouldn't. Birds are somewhat

stupid creatures and have a hard enough job even coming to terms with the ordinary, let alone the extraordinary. But if it had been an unusually intelligent bird—an escaped myna bird, perhaps, or a parrot that had been blown several thousand miles off course by very strong winds—it would have thought:

Oh. There is a wide hole in the hill, with little old rusty sheds in it, and a fence in front of it.

And there is a car with lights on the top of it just going through a gate in the fence.

And there are little black dots on the ground ahead of it. One dot standing very still, right in the path of the thing, and the others, the others . . .

Breaking away and running. Running for their lives.

They never did find Nisodemus again, even though a party of strong-stomached nomes went back much later and searched through the ruts and the mud.

So a rumor grew up that perhaps, at the last minute, he had jumped up and caught hold of part of the car and had clambered onto it somehow. And then he'd waited there, too ashamed to face other nomes, until the car went back to wherever it came from, and had got off, and was living out the rest of his life quietly and without any fuss. He had been a good nome in his way, they said. Whatever else you might say about him, he believed in things and he did what he thought was proper, so it was only right that he'd been spared and was still out there in the world, somewhere.

This was what they told one another, and what they wrote down in the Book of Nome.

What nomes might have thought in those private moments before they went to sleep . . . well, that was private.

Humans clomped slowly around the train and what remained of the truck. Lots of other vehicles had turned up at what was, for humans, great speed. Many of them had lights on top.

The nomes had learned to be worried by things with flashing lights on top.

The Land-Rover belonging to the quarrymen was there as well. One of the quarrymen was pointing to the wrecked truck and shouting at the others. It had opened the smashed engine compartment, and was pointing to where the battery wasn't.

Beside the railroad the breeze rustled the long grass. And some of the long grass rustled without any wind at all.

Dorcas had been right. Where humans went once, they went again. The quarry belonged to them. Three trucks were parked outside the sheds and humans were everywhere. Some were repairing the fence. Some were taking boxes and drums off trucks. One was even in the manager's office, cleaning up.

The nomes crouched where they could, listening fearfully to the sounds above them. There weren't many hiding places for two thousand nomes, small though they were.

It was a very long day. In the shadows under some of the sheds, in the darkness behind crates, in some cases even on the dusty rafters under the tin roofs, the nomes passed it as best they could.

There were escapes so narrow a postcard couldn't have got through them. Old Munby Confectioneri and most of his family were left blinking in the light when a human moved the beat-up old box they were cowering behind. Only a quick dash to the shelter of a stack of cans saved them. And, of course, the fact that humans never really looked hard at what they were doing.

That wasn't the worst part, though.

The worst part was much worse.

The nomes sat in the noisy darkness, not daring even to speak, and felt their world vanishing. Not because the humans hated nomes. *Because they didn't notice them.*

There was Dorcas's electricity, for example. He'd spent a long time twisting bits of wire together and finding a safe way to steal electricity from the fusebox. A human pulled the wire bits out without thinking, fiddled inside with a screwdriver, and then put up a new box with a lock on it.

The Store nomes needed electricity. They couldn't remember a time when they had been without it. It was a natural thing, like air. And now theirs was a world of endless darkness.

And still the terror went on. The rough floor-boards shook overhead, raining dust and splinters. Metal drums boomed like thunder. There was the continual sound of hammering. The humans were back, and they meant to stay.

They did go eventually, though. When the day-light drained from the winter sky, like steel grow-ing cold, some of the humans got into their vehicles and drove off down the dirt road.

They did one puzzling thing before they left. Nomes had to scramble over one another to get out of the way when one of the floorboards in the man-ager's office was pulled up. A huge hand reached down and put a little tray on the packed earth un-der the floor. Then the darkness came back as the board was replaced.

The nomes sat in the gloom and wondered why on earth the humans, after a day like this, were giving them food.

The tray was piled with flour. It wasn't much, compared to Store food, but to nomes who had spent all day hungry and miserable it smelled *good*.

A couple of younger ones crawled closer. It had the most tantalizing smell.

One of them took a handful of the stuff.

"Don't eat it!"

Grimma pushed her way through the packed bodies.

"But it smells so—" one of the nomes warbled.

"Have you ever smelled anything like it before?" she said.

"Well, no—"

"So you don't *know* it's good to eat, do you? Listen. I know about stuff like this. Where we—where I used to live, in the hole . . . there was a place along the highway where humans came to eat, and sometimes we'd find stuff like this among the trash at the back. It kills you if you eat it!"

The nomes looked at the innocent little tray. Food that killed you? That didn't make sense.

"I remember there was some canned meat we had once in the Store," said an elderly nome. "Gave us all a nasty upset, I remember." He gave Grimma a hopeful look.

She shook her head. "This isn't like that," she said. "We used to find dead rats near it. They didn't die in a very nice way," she added, shuddering at the memory.

"Oh."

The nomes stared at the tray again. And there was a thump from overhead.

There was still a human in the quarry.

It was sitting in the old swivel chair in the manager's office, reading a paper.

From a knothole near the floor the nomes watched carefully. There were huge boots, great sweeps of trouser, a mountain range of jacket and, far above, the distant gleam of electric light on a bald head.

After a long while the human put the paper down and reached over to the desk by its side. The watching nomes gazed at a pack of sandwiches bigger than they were, and a Thermos flask that steamed when it was opened and filled the shed with the smell of soup.

They climbed back down and reported to Grimma. She was sitting by the food tray, and had ordered six of the older and more sensible nomes to stand guard around it to keep children away.

"It's not doing anything," she was told. "It's just sitting there. We saw it look out of the window once or twice."

"Then it'll be here all night," said Grimma. "I expect the humans are wondering who's causing all this trouble."

"What shall we *do*?"

Grimma sat with her chin on her hands.

"There's those big old tumbledown sheds across the quarry," she said at last. "We could go there."

"Dorcas said—Dorcas used to say it was very dangerous in the old sheds," said a nome cautiously. "Because of all the old metal and stuff. Very dangerous, he said."

"More dangerous than here?" said Grimma, with just a trace of her old sarcasm.

"You've got a point."

"Please, ma'am."

It was one of the younger female nomes. They held Grimma in awe because of the way she shouted at the men and read better than anyone.

This one held a baby in her arms, and kept curtsying every time she finished a sentence.

"What it is, Sorrit?" said Grimma.

"Please, ma'am, some of the children are very hungry, ma'am. There isn't anything wholesome to eat down here, you see." She gave Grimma a pleading look.

Grimma nodded. The stores were under the other sheds, what was left of them. The main potato store had been found by some of the humans, which was perhaps why the poison had been put down. Anyway, they couldn't light a fire and there was no meat. No one had been doing any proper hunting for *days*, because Arnold Bros. (est. 1905) would provide, according to Nisodemus.

"As soon as it gets light I think all the hunters we can spare should go out," said Grimma.

They considered this. The dawn was a long way away. To a nome, a night was as long as three whole days.

"There's plenty of snow," said a nome. "That means we've got water."

"We might be able to manage without food, but the children won't," said Grimma.

"And the old people too," said a nome. "It's going to freeze again tonight. We haven't got the electric and we can't light a fire outside."

They sat staring glumly at the dirt.

What Grimma was thinking was: They're not bickering. They're not grumbling. Things are so serious they're actually not arguing and blaming each other.

"All right," she said. "And what do *you* all think we should do?"

Eleven

I. We will come out of the woodwork.
II. We will come out of the floor.
III. They will wish they had never seen us.
   —From the *Book of Nome, Humans I, v. I–III*

The human lowered its newspaper and listened.

There was a rustling in the walls. There was a scratching under the floor.

Its eyes swivelled to the table beside it.

A group of small creatures were dragging its packet of sandwiches across the tabletop. It blinked.

Then it roared and tried to stand up, and it wasn't until it was nearly upright that it found that its feet were tied very firmly to the legs of its chair.

It crashed forward. A crowd of tiny creatures, moving so fast that it could hardly see them, charged out from under the table and wrapped a length of old electrical wire around its outflung arms. Within seconds it was trussed awkwardly, but very firmly, between the furniture.

They saw its great eyes roll. It opened its mouth and mooed at them. Teeth like yellow plates clashed at them.

The wire held.

The sandwiches turned out to be cheese and pickle and the Thermos, once they got the top off, was full of coffee. "Store food," said one nome to another. "Good Store food, like we used to know."

They poured into the room from every crack and mousehole. There was an electric fire by the table and they sat in solemn rows in front of its glowing red bar or wandered around the crowded office.

"We done it," they said, "Just like that *Gullible Travels*. The bigger they come, the harder they fall!"

There was a school of thought that said they should kill the human, whose mad eyes followed them around the floor. This was when they found the box.

It was on one of the shelves. It was yellow. It had a picture of a very unhappy-looking rat on the front. It had the word Scramoff in big red lettering too. On the back . . .

Grimma's forehead wrinkled as she tried to read the smaller words on the back.

"It says, 'They Take a Bite, but They Don't Come Back for More!' " she said. "And apparently it contains polydichloromethylinlon-4, whatever that is. 'Clears Outhouses of Troublesome . . .' " She paused.

"Troublesome what?" said the listening nomes. "Troublesome what?"

Grimma lowered her voice.

"It says, 'Clears Outhouses of Troublesome *Vermin* in a Trice!' " she said. "It's poison. It's the stuff they put under the floor."

The silence that followed this was black with rage. The nomes had raised quite a lot of children in the quarry. They had very firm views about poison.

"We should make the human eat it," said one of them. "Fill up its mouth with Polypuththeketlon or whatever it is. Troublesome *vermin.*"

"I think they think we're rats," said Grimma.

"And that would be all right, would it?" said a nome with withering sarcasm. "Rats are okay. We've never had any trouble with rats. No call to go around giving them poisoned food."

In fact, the nomes got on rather well with the local rats, probably because their leader was Bobo, who had been a pet of Angalo's when they lived in the Store. The two species treated each other with the distant friendliness of creatures who could, at a pinch, eat one another but had decided not to.

"Yeah, the rats'd thank us for getting rid of a human," he went on.

"No," said Grimma. "No. I don't think we should do that. Dorcas always said that they're nearly as intelligent as we are. You can't go around poisoning intelligent creatures."

"*They* tried!"

"They're not nomes. They don't know how to behave," said Grimma. "Anyway, be sensible. More humans will come along in the morning. If they find a dead human, there'll be a lot of trouble."

That was a point. But they had shown themselves to a human. No nome could remember its ever being done before. They'd had to do it, or starve and freeze, but there was no knowing where it would end. *How* it would end was a bit more certain. It would probably end badly.

"Go and put it somewhere where the rats can't get it," said Grimma.

"I reckon we should just give it a taste—" said the nome.

"No! Just take the stuff away. We'll stay here the rest of the night and then move out before it's light."

"Well, all right. If you say so. I just hope we're not sorry about it later, that's all." The nomes carried the dreadful box away.

Grimma wandered over to where the human lay. It was well trussed up by now, and couldn't move a finger. It looked just like the picture of Gullible or whoever he was, except the nomes had got hold of what the nomes in those days had never heard of, which was lots of electrical wire. It was a lot tougher than rope. And they were a lot angrier. Gullible hadn't been driving a great big truck around the place and putting down rat poison.

They'd gone through its pockets and piled up the

contents in a heap. There'd been a big square of white cloth among them, which a group of nomes had managed to tie around the human's mouth after its mooing got on everyone's nerves.

Now they stood around eating pieces of bread and cheese and pickle and watching the human's eyes.

Humans can't understand nomes. Their voices are too fast and too high, like a bat squeak. It was probably just as well.

"*I* say we should find something sharp and stick it into it," said a nome. "In all the soft parts."

"There's things we could do with matches," said Granny Morkie, to Grimma's surprise.

"And nails," said a middle-aged nome.

The human growled behind its gag and strained at the wires.

"We could pull all its hair out," said Granny Morkie. "And then we could—"

"Do it, then," said Grimma, coming up behind them.

They turned.

"What?"

"Do it, if you want to," said Grimma. "There it is, right in front of you. Do what you like."

"What, *me*?" Granny Morkie nome drew back. "I didn't . . . not *me*. I didn't mean *me*. I meant . . . well, us. Nomekind."

"There you are, then," said Grimma. "And nomekind is only nomes. Besides, it's wrong to hurt prisoners. I read it in a book. It's called the

Geneva Convention. When you've got people at your mercy, you shouldn't hurt them."

"Seems like the ideal time to me," said a nome. "Hit them when they can't hit back, that's what I say. Anyway, it's not as if humans are the same as real people." But he shuffled backward anyway.

"Funny, though, when you see their faces close up," said Granny Morkie, putting her head to one side. "They look a lot like us. Only bigger."

One of the nomes peered into the human's frightened eyes.

"Hasn't it got a hairy nose?" he said. "And ears too."

"Like a cow," said Granny.

"You could almost feel sorry for them, with great big noses like that."

Grimma peered into the human's eyes. I wonder, she thought. They're bigger than us, so there must be room for brains. And they've got great big eyes. Surely they must have seen us once? Masklin said we've been here for thousands of years. In all that time, humans must have seen us.

They must have known we were real people. But in their minds they turned us into pixies. Perhaps they didn't want to have to share the world.

The human was definitely looking at her.

Could we share? she thought. They live in a big, long, slow world and we live in a small, short, fast one, and we can't understand each other. They can't even see us unless we stand still as I'm standing now. We move too quickly for them. They don't think we exist.

She stared up into the big frightened eyes.

We've never tried to—what was the word—*communicate* with them before. Not properly. Not as though they were real people, thinking real thoughts. How can we tell them we're really real and really here?

But perhaps when you're lying down on the floor and tied up by little people you can hardly see and don't believe in, that's not the best time to start communicating. Perhaps we should try it another time. Not signs, not shouting, just trying to get them to understand us.

Wouldn't it be amazing if we could? They could do the big slow jobs for us, and we could do—oh, little fast things. Fiddly things that those great fingers can't do . . . but not paint flowers or mend their shoes.

"Grimma? You ought to see this, Grimma," said a voice behind her.

The nomes were clustered around a white heap on the floor.

Oh, yes. The human had been looking at one of those big sheets of paper.

The nomes had spread it out flat on the floor. It looked a lot like the first one they'd seen, except this one was called READ IT FIRST IN YOUR SOARAWAY BLACKBURY EVENING POST AND GAZETTE. It had more of the great blocky writing, some of the letters nearly as big as a nome's head.

Grimma shook her own head as she tried to make sense of it. She could understand the books quite well, she considered, but the papers seemed to use a different language. It was full of *probes* and *shocks* and fuzzy pictures of smiling humans shaking hands with other humans (ELKS RAISE £455 FOR HOSPITAL APPEAL). It wasn't difficult to work out what each word meant, but when they were put together they either didn't mean anything at all or something quite unbelievable (CIVIC CENTER TAX BATTLE).

"No, this is the bit," said one of the nomes. "This page here. Look, some of the words, they're the same as last time, look! *It's about Grandson Richard, 39!*"

Grimma ran the length of a story about somebody slamming somebody's plan for something.

There was indeed a fuzzy picture of Grandson Richard, 39, under the words: TV-IN-THE-SKY HITCH.

She knelt down and stared at the smaller words below it.

"Read it aloud!" they said.

" 'Richard Arnold, the Blackbury-based chairman of the Arnco International Group, said in Florida today,' " she read, " 'that scientists are still trying to r-r-regain control of Arnsat 1, the multi-million-pound com . . . communications sat . . . tellite . . .' "

The nomes looked at one another.

"Multimillion pound," they said, "That's really heavy."

" 'Hopes were high after yesterday's s-s-successful l-lunch in Florida,' " Grimma read uncertainly, " 'that Arnsat 1 would begin test tr-tr-transmissions today. Instead, it is s-sending a stream of strange sig . . . signals. "It's like some sort of c-code," said Arnold, 39 . . ."' ' "

There was an appreciative murmur from the listeners.

" 'It's as if it had a mind of its own,' " Grimma read.

There was more stuff about "teething troubles," whatever that meant, but Grimma didn't bother to read it.

She remembered the way Masklin had talked about the stars, and why they stayed up. And there was the Thing. He'd taken it with him. The Thing could talk to electricity, couldn't it? It could listen to the electricity in wires, and the stuff in the air that Dorcas called "radio." If anything could send strange signals, the Thing could. *I may go even further than the Long Drive,* he'd said.

"They're alive," she said, to no one in particular. "Masklin and Gurder and Angalo. They got to the Florida place and they're alive."

She remembered him trying to tell her, sometimes, about the sky and the Thing and where nomes first came from, and she'd never really understood, any more than he'd understood about the little frogs.

"They're alive," she repeated. "I know they are. I don't know exactly how or where, but they've got some sort of plan and they're alive."

The nomes exchanged meaningful glances, and the kind of meaning they were full of was, She's fooling herself, but it'd take a braver nome than *me* to tell her.

Granny Morkie patted her gently on the shoulder.

"Yes, yes," she said soothingly. "And thank goodness they had a successful lunch. I bet they needed to get some food inside of them. And if I was you, my girl, I'd get some sleep."

Grimma dreamed.

It was a confused dream. Dreams nearly always are. They don't come neatly packaged. She dreamed of loud noises and flashing lights. And eyes.

Little yellow eyes. And Masklin, standing on a branch, climbing through leaves, peering down at little yellow eyes.

I'm seeing what he's doing now, she thought. *He's alive. I always knew he was, of course. But outer space has got more leaves than I thought. Or perhaps none of it is real and I'm just dreaming . . .*

Then someone woke her up.

It's never wise to speculate about the meaning of dreams, so she didn't.

It snowed again in the night, on an icy wind. Some of the nomes scouted around the sheds and came back with a few vegetables that had been missed, but it was a pitifully small amount. The tied-up human went to sleep after a while, and snored like someone sawing a thick log with a thin saw.

"The others will come looking for it in the morning," Grimma warned. "We mustn't be here then. Perhaps we should—"

She stopped. They all listened.

Something was moving around under the floorboards.

"Is anyone still down there?" Grimma whispered.

The nomes near her shook their heads. No one wanted to be in the chilly space under the floor when there was the warmth and light of the office for the having.

"And it can't be rats," she said.

Then someone called out in that half-loud, half-soft way of someone who wants to make himself heard while at the same time remaining as quiet as possible.

It turned out to be Sacco.

They dragged aside the floorboards the humans had loosened and helped him up. He was covered in mud and swaying with exhaustion.

"I couldn't find anyone!" he gasped. "I looked everywhere and I couldn't find anyone and we saw the trucks come here and I saw the lights on and I thought the humans were still here and I came in and I heard your voices and you've got to come because it's Dorcas!"

"He's alive?" said Grimma.

"If he isn't, he can swear pretty well for a dead person," said Sacco, sagging to the floor.

"We thought you were all de—" Grimma began.

"We're all fine except for Dorcas. He hurt himself jumping out of the truck! Come on, *please!*"

"You don't look in any state to go anywhere," said Grimma. She stood up. "You just tell us where he is."

"We got him halfway up the road and we got so tired and I left them and came on ahead," Sacco blurted out. "They're under the hedge and—" His eyes fell on the snoring bulk of the human. He stared at Grimma.

"You've captured a *human?*" he said. He stumbled sideways. "Need a bit of a rest. So tired. So tired," he repeated, vaguely. Then he fell forward.

Grimma caught him and laid him down as gently as she could.

"Someone put him somewhere warm and see if there's any food left," she said to the nomes in general. "And I want some of you to help me look for the others. Come on. This isn't a night for being outside."

The expression on the faces of some of the nomes said that they definitely agreed with this point of view, and that among the people who shouldn't be out on a night like this was themselves.

"It's snowing quite a lot," said one of them, uncertainly. "We'll never find them in all the dark and snow."

Grimma glared at him.

"We might," she said. "We *might* find them in all the dark and snow. We *won't* find them by staying in the light and warm, I know that much."

Several nomes pushed their way forward. Grimma recognized Nooty's people, and the parents of some of the lads. Then there was a bit of a commotion from under the table, where the oldest nomes were clustering together to keep warm and have a good moan.

"I'm comin' too," said Granny Morkie. "Do me good to have a drop of fresh air. What you all lookin' at me like that for?"

"I think you ought to stay inside, Granny," said Grimma gently.

"Don't you come the bein'-tactful-to-old-people to me, my gel," said Granny, prodding her with her stick. "I bin out in deep snow before you was even thought of." She turned to the rest of the nomes. "Nothin' to it if you acts sensible and keeps yellin' out so's everyone knows where everyone is. I went out to help look for my uncle Joe before I was a year old," she said, proudly. "Dreadful snow, that was. It come down sudden, like, when the men were out huntin'. We found nearly all of him too."

"Yes, yes, all right, Granny," said Grimma quickly. She looked at the others. "Well, *we're* going," she said.

In the end fifteen of them went, many out of sheer embarrassment.

In the yellow light from the shed windows the

snowflakes looked beautiful. By the time they reached the ground they were pretty unpleasant.

The Store nomes really *hated* the Outside snow. There had been snow in the Store, too, sprayed on merchandise around Christmas Fayre time. But it wasn't cold. And snowflakes were huge beautiful things that were hung from the ceilings on bits of thread. *Proper* snowflakes. Not ghastly things which looked all right in the air but turned into freezing wet stuff which was allowed to just lie around on the floor.

It already was deep as their knees.

"What you do is," said Granny Morkie, "you lift your feet up really high and plonk them down. Nothin' to it."

The light from the shed shone out across the quarry, but the dirt road was a dark tunnel leading into the night.

"And spread out," said Grimma. "But keep together."

"Spread out and keep together," they muttered.

A senior nome put his hand up.

"You don't get *robins* at night, do you?" he asked cautiously.

"No, of course not," said Grimma.

"No, you don't get robins at night, silly," said Granny Morkie.

They looked relieved.

"No, you get foxes," Granny added, in a self-satisfied way. "Great big foxes. They get good and hungry in the cold weather. And maybe you get owls." She scratched her chin. "Cunnin' devils, owls. You never hear 'em till they're almost on top o' you." She banged on the wall with her stick. "Look sharp, you lot. Best foot forward. Unless you're like my uncle Joe—a fox got 'is best foot, 'e 'ad to have a wooden leg, 'e was livid."

There was something about Granny Morkie's cheering people up that always got them moving. Anything was better than being cheered up some more.

The snowflakes were caking up on the dried grasses and ferns on either bank. Every now and again some of it fell off, sometimes onto the dirt road, often onto the nomes stumbling along it. They prodded the snowy tussocks and peered doubtfully into the gloomy holes under the hedge, while the flakes continued to fall in a soft, crackly silence. Robins, owls, and other terrors of the Outside lurked in every shadow.

Eventually the light was left behind and they walked by the glow of the snow itself. Sometimes one of them would call out, softly, and then they'd all listen.

It was very cold.

Granny Morkie stopped suddenly.

"Fox," she announced. "I can smell it. Can't mistake a fox. *Rank.*"

They huddled together and stared apprehensively into the darkness.

"Might not still be around, mind," said Granny. "Hangs about for a long time, that smell."

They relaxed a bit.

"Really, Granny," muttered Grimma.

"I was just tryin' to be a help," sniffed Granny Morkie. "You don't want my help, you've only got to say."

"We're doing this wrong," said Grimma. "It's *Dorcas* we're looking for. He wouldn't just be sitting out in the open, would he? He knows about foxes. He'd get the boys to find somewhere sheltered and as safe as possible."

Nooty's father stepped forward.

"If you look the way the snow falls," he said hesitantly, "you can see the air conditioning is blowing it *this* way." He pointed. "So it piles up more on this side of things than that side. So they'd want to be as much away from the air conditioning as possible, wouldn't they?"

"It's called the wind, when it's Outside," said Grimma gently. "But you're right. That means"— she peered at the hedges—"they'd be on the other side of the hedge. In the field, up against the bank. Come on."

They scrambled up through the masses of dead leaves and dripping twigs and into the field beyond.

It was desolate. A few tufts of dead grass stuck above the endless wilderness of snow. Several of the nomes groaned.

It's the size, Grimma thought. They don't mind the quarry, or the thickets above it, or even the road, because a lot of it is closed in and you can pretend there are sort of walls around you. It's too *big* for them here.

"Stick close to the hedge," she said, more cheerfully than she felt. "There's not so much snow there."

Oh, Arnold Bros. (est. 1905), she thought. Dorcas doesn't believe in you, and I certainly don't believe in you, but if you could just see your way clear to existing just long enough for us to find them, we'd all appreciate it very much. And perhaps if you could stop the snow and see us all safely back to the quarry as well, that would be a big help.

That's crazy, she thought. Masklin always said that if there was an Arnold Bros., he was sort of inside our heads, helping us think.

She realized that she was staring at the snow.

Why is there a hole in it? she thought.

Twelve

IV.   There is nowhere to go, and we must go.
    —From the *Book of Nome, Exits III, v. IV*

"Rabbits, I thought," she said.

Dorcas patted her hand.

"Well done," he said weakly.

"We were on the road after Sacco left," said Nooty, "and it was getting really cold and Dorcas said to take him to the other side of the hedge and, well, it was me who said you can see rabbits in this field sometimes, and *he* said find a rabbit hole. So we did. We thought we'd be here all night."

"Ow," moaned Dorcas.

"Don't make a fuss, I didn't hurt a bit," said Granny Morkie cheerfully, as she examined his leg. "Nothin' broken, but it's a nasty sprain."

The Store nomes looked around the burrow with interest and a certain amount of approval. It was nicely closed in.

"Your ancestors probably lived in holes like

this," said Grimma. "With shelves and things, of course."

"Very nice," said a nome. "Homey. Almost like being under the floor."

"Stinks a bit," said another.

"That'll be the rabbits," said Dorcas, nodding toward the deeper darkness. "We've heard them rustling about, but they're staying out of our way. Nooty said he thought there was a fox snuffling around a while ago."

"We'd better get you back as soon as possible," said Grimma. "I don't *think* any fox would bother the pack of us. After all, the local ones know who we are. Eat a nome and you die, that's what they've learned."

The nomes shuffled their feet. It was true, of course. The trouble *was,* they thought, that the person who'd really regret it the most would be the one nome who was eaten. Knowing that the fox might be given a bad time afterward wouldn't be much consolation.

Besides, they were cold and wet and the burrow, while it wouldn't have sounded like a very comfortable proposition back at the quarry, was suddenly much better than the horrible night outside. They'd staggered past a dozen burrows, calling down into the gloom, before they'd heard Nooty's voice answering them.

"I really don't think we need worry," said Grimma. "Foxes learn very quickly. Isn't that so, Granny?"

"Eh?" said Granny Morkie.

"I was telling everyone how foxes learn quickly," said Grimma desperately.

"Oh, yes. Right enough," said Granny. "He'll go a long way out of his way for something he likes to eat, will your average fox. Especially when it's cold weather."

"I didn't mean that! Why do you have to make everything sound so *bad*?"

"I'm sure I don't mean to," said Granny Morkie, and sniffed.

"We must get back," said Dorcas firmly. "This snow isn't just going to go away, is it? I can get along okay if I've got someone to lean on."

"We can make you a stretcher," said Grimma. "Though goodness knows there isn't much to get back *to.*"

"We saw the humans go up the road," said Nooty. "But we had to go all the way along to the badger tunnel and there were no real paths. Then we tried to cut across the fields at the bottom and that was a mistake, they were all plowed up. We haven't had anything to eat," he added.

"Don't expect much, then," said Grimma. "The humans took most of our supplies. They think we're rats."

"Well, that's not so bad," said Dorcas. "We used to encourage them to think we were, back in the Store. They used to put traps down. We used to hunt rats in the basement and put them in the traps, when I was a lad."

"Now they're using poisoned food," said Grimma.

"That's not good."

"Come on. Let's get you back."

The snow was still falling outside, but raggedy fashion, as if the last flakes in stock were being sold off cheaply. There was a line of red light in the east —not the dawn, but the promise of the dawn. It didn't look cheerful. When the sun did rise, it would find itself locked behind bars of cloud.

They broke off some pieces of dead cow-parsley stalks to make a rough sort of chair for Dorcas, which four nomes could carry. He'd been right about the shelter of the hedge. The snow wasn't very deep there, but it made up for it by being littered with old leaves, twigs, and debris. It was slow going.

It must be great to be a human, Grimma thought as thorns the length of her hand tore at her dress. Masklin was right, this really is their world. It's the right size for them. They go where they want and do whatever they like. We think we do things for ourselves and all we do is live in odd corners of their world—under their floors, stealing things.

The other nomes trudged along in weary silence. The only sound, apart from the crunch of feet on snow and leaves, was that of Granny Morkie eating. She'd found some hawthorn berries on a bush and was chewing her way through one with every sign of enjoyment. She'd offered them around, but the other nomes found them bitter and unpleasant.

"Prob'ly an acquired taste," she muttered, glaring at Grimma.

It's one we all are going to have to acquire, thought Grimma, ignoring Granny's hurt stare. The only hope we've got is to split up and leave the quarry in little groups, once we get back. Move out into the country, go back to living in old rabbit holes and eating whatever we can find. Some groups may survive the winter, once the old people have died off.

And it'll be good-bye electricity, good-bye reading, good-bye bananas . . .

But I'll wait at the quarry until Masklin comes back.

"Cheer up, my girl," said Granny Morkie, trying to be friendly. "Don't look so gloomy. It may never happen, that's what I always say."

Even Granny was shocked when Grimma looked at her with a face from which all the color had drained away. The girl's mouth opened and shut a few times.

Then she folded up, very gently, and collapsed to her knees and started to sob.

It was the most shocking sound they'd heard. Grimma yelled, complained, bullied, and commanded. Hearing her cry was *wrong*, as though the whole world had turned upside down.

"All I did was try to cheer her up," mumbled Granny Morkie.

The embarrassed nomes stood around in a circle. No one dared go near Grimma. Anything might happen. If you tried to pat her on the shoulder and say "There, there," anything might happen. She might bite your hand off, or anything.

Dorcas looked at the nomes on either side of him, sighed, and eased himself up off his makeshift stretcher. He limped over to Grimma, catching hold of a thorn twig to steady himself.

"You've found us, we're going back to the quarry, everything's all right," he said soothingly.

"It isn't! We'll have to move on!" she sobbed. "You'd have been better off staying in the hole! It's all gone bad!"

"Well, I would have said—" Dorcas began.

"We've got no food and we can't stop the humans and we're trapped in the quarry and I've tried to keep everyone together and now it's all gone bad!"

"We ought to have gone up to that barn right at the start," said Nooty.

"You still could," said Grimma. "All the younger people could. Just get as far away from here as possible!"

"But children couldn't walk it, and old people certainly couldn't manage the snow," said Dorcas. "*You* know that. You're just despairing."

"We've tried everything! It's just got worse! We thought it would be a lovely life in the Outside and now it's all falling to pieces!"

Dorcas gave her a long, blank look.

"We might as well give up right now," she said. "We might as well give up and die right here."

There was a horrified silence.

It was broken by Dorcas.

"Er," he said. "Er. Are you sure? Are you *really* sure?"

The tone of his voice made Grimma look up.

All the nomes were staring.

There was a fox looking down at them.

It was one of those moments when Time itself freezes solid. Grimma could see the yellow-green glow in the fox's eyes and the cloud of its breath. Its tongue lolled out.

It looked surprised.

It was new to these parts and had never seen nomes before. Its not-very-complicated mind was trying to come to terms with the fact that the *shape* of the nomes—two arms, two legs, a head at the top—was a shape it associated with humans and had learned to avoid, but the size was the size it had always thought of as a mouthful.

The nomes stood rooted in terror. There was no sense in trying to run away. A fox had twice as many legs to run after you. You'd end up dead anyway, but at least you wouldn't end up dead and out of breath as well.

There was a growl.

To the nomes' astonishment, it had come from Grimma.

She snatched Granny Morkie's walking stick, strode forward, and whacked the fox across the nose before it could move. It yelped and blinked stupidly.

"Shove off!" she shouted. "How dare you come here!" She hit it again. It jerked its head away.

Grimma took another step forward and caught it a backward thump across the muzzle.

The fox made up its mind. There were definitely rabbits further down the hedge. Rabbits didn't hit back. It knew where it was with rabbits.

It whined, backed away with its eyes fixed on Grimma, and then darted off into the darkness.

The nomes breathed out.

"*Well,*" said Dorcas.

"I'm sorry, but I just can't *stand* foxes," said Grimma. "And Masklin said we should let them know who's boss."

"I'm not arguing," said Dorcas.

Grimma looked vaguely at the stick.

"What was I saying before that?" she said.

"You were saying we might as well give up and die right here," said Granny Morkie helpfully. Grimma glared at her.

"No I wasn't," she said. "I was just feeling a bit tired, that's all. Come on. We'll catch our death standing here."

"Or the other way around," said Sacco, staring into the fox-haunted darkness.

"That's not funny," snapped Grimma, striding off.

"I didn't mean it to be," said Sacco, shivering.

Overhead, quite unnoticed by the nomes, a rather strangely bright star zigzagged across the sky. It was small, or perhaps it was really very big but a long way off. If you looked at it long enough, it might just appear disc-shaped. It was causing a lot of messages to be sent through the air, all around the world.

It seemed to be looking for something.

There were flickering lights in the quarry by the time they got back. Another group of nomes was about to set out to look for them. Not with much enthusiasm, admittedly, but they were going to try.

The cheer that went up when it was realized that everyone was back safely almost made Grimma forget that they were safely back to a very unsafe place. She'd read something in the book of proverbs that summed it up perfectly. As far as she could remember, it was something about jumping out of the thing you cook in and into the thing you cooked on. Or something.

Grimma led the rescue party into the office and listened while Sacco, with many interruptions, recounted the adventure from the time Dorcas, out of sudden terror, had jumped out of the truck and had been carried off the rails just before the train arrived. It sounded brave and exciting. And pointless, Grimma thought, but she kept that to herself.

"It wasn't as bad as it looked," Sacco said. "I mean, the truck was smashed but the train didn't even come off the rails. We saw it all," he finished. "I'm starving."

He gave them a bright smile, which faded like a sunset.

"There's no food?" he said.

"Even less than that," said a nome. "If you've got some bread, we could have a snow sandwich."

Sacco thought about this.

"There's the rabbits," he said. "There were rabbits in the field."

"And in the dark," said Dorcas, who appeared to have something on his mind.

"Well, yes," admitted Sacco.

"And with that fox hanging about," said Nooty.

Another proverb floated up in Grimma's mind.

"Needs must," she said, "when the Devil drives."

They looked at her in the flickering light of the matches.

"Who's he?" said Nooty.

"Some sort of horrible person that lives under the ground in a hot place, I think," said Grimma.

"Like the boiler room in the Store?"

"I suppose so."

"And what sort of vehicle does he drive?" said Sacco, looking interested.

"It just means that sometimes you're forced to do things," said Grimma testily. "I don't think he actually *drives* anything."

"Well, no. There wouldn't be the room down there, for one thing."

Dorcas coughed. He seemed to be upset about something. Well, everyone was upset, but he was even more upset.

"All right," he said quietly.

Something about the way he said it made them pay attention.

"You'd all better come with me," he went on. "Believe me, I'd rather you didn't have to."

"Where to?" said Grimma.

"The old sheds. The ones by the cliff," said Dorcas.

"But they're all tumbled down. And you said they were very dangerous."

"Oh, they are. They are. There's piles of junk and stuff in cans the children shouldn't touch and stuff like that."

He twiddled his beard nervously.

"But," he said, "there's something else. Something I've been sort of working on, sort of."

He looked her in the eye. "Something of mine," he said. "The most marvellous thing I've ever seen. Even better than frogs in a flower."

Then he coughed. "Anyway, there's plenty of room in there," he said. "The floors are just earth, er, but the sheds are big and there are lots of places, er, to hide."

A snore from the human shook the office.

"Besides, I don't like being so close to that thing," he added.

There was a general murmur of agreement about this.

"Had you thought about what you're going to do with it?" said Dorcas.

"Some people wanted to kill it, but I don't think that's a good idea," said Grimma. "I think the other humans would get really upset about it."

"Besides, it doesn't seem right," said Dorcas.

"I know what you mean."

"So . . . what shall we do with it?"

Grimma glared at the huge face. Every pore, every hair, was huge. It was strange to think that if there were creatures smaller than nomes, little people perhaps the size of ants, her own face might look like that. If you looked at it philosophically, the whole thing about big and small was just a matter of size.

"We'll leave it," she said. "But . . . is there any paper here?"

"Loads of it on the desk," said Nooty.

"Go and fetch some, please. Dorcas, you've always got something to write with, haven't you?"

Dorcas fumbled in his pockets until he found a stub of pencil lead.

"Don't waste it," he said. "Don't know if I'll ever get any more."

Eventually Nooty came back towing a yellowing sheet of paper. At the top of it, in heavy black lettering, were the words BLACKBURY SAND AND GRAVEL INC. Below that was the word INVOICE.

Grimma thought for a while, and then licked the stub and, in big letters, started to write.

"What are you doing?" said Dorcas.

"Trying to communicate," said Grimma. She carefully traced another word, pressing quite hard.

"I've always thought it might be worth trying," said Dorcas. "But is this the right time?"

"Yes," said Grimma. She finished the last word.

"What do you think?" she said, handing Dorcas the pencil lead.

The writing was a bit jagged where she had pressed hard, and her grasp of grammar and writing wasn't as good as her skill at reading, but it was clear enough.

"I would have done it differently," said Dorcas, reading it.

"Perhaps you would, but this is the way *I've* done it."

"Yes." Dorcas put his head on one side. "Well, it's definitely a communication. You can't get much more communicating than that. Yes."

Grimma tried to sound cheerful. "And now," she said, "Let's see this shed of yours."

Two minutes later the office shed was empty of nomes. The human snored on the floor, one hand outstretched.

There was a piece of paper in it now.

It said: BLACKBURY SAND AND GRAVEL INC.

It said: INVOICE.

It said: We Could of Kiled You. LEAV US ALONE.

Now it was quite light outside, and the snow had stopped.

"They'll see our tracks," said Sacco. "Even humans will notice this many tracks."

"It doesn't matter," said Dorcas. "Just get everyone into the old sheds."

"Are you sure, Dorcas?" said Grimma. "Are you really *sure* this is a good idea?"

"No."

They joined the stream of nomes hurrying through a crack in the crumbling corrugated metal and entered the vast, echoing chamber of the shed.

Grimma looked around her. Rust and time had eaten large holes in the walls and ceiling. Old cans and coils of wire were stacked willy-nilly in the corners, along with odd-shaped bits of metal and jam jars with nails in them. Everything stank of oil.

"What's the part we ought to know about?" she said.

Dorcas pointed to the shadows at the far end of the shed, where she could just make out something big and indistinct.

"It just looks like . . . some sort of big cloth . . ." she said.

"It's, um, underneath it. Is everyone in?" Dorcas cupped his hands around his mouth. "*Is everyone in?*" he shouted. He turned to Nooty.

"I need to know where everyone is," he said. "I don't want anyone to be frightened, but I don't want unnecessary people getting in the way."

"Unnecessary for what?" said Grimma, but he ignored her.

"Sacco, you take some of the lads and get those things we put in the hedge," said Dorcas. "We'll definitely need the battery and I'm really not certain how much fuel there is."

"*Dorcas!* What is it?" said Grimma, tapping her foot.

Dorcas got like this sometimes, she knew. When he was thinking about machines or things he could do with his hands, he started to ignore people. His voice changed too.

He gave her a long, slow look as if he were seeing her for the first time. Then he looked down at his feet.

"You'd better, er, come and see," he said. "I shall need you to explain things to everyone. You're so much better at that sort of thing."

Grimma followed him across the chilly floor as more nomes filed into the shed and huddled apprehensively along the walls.

He led her under the shadow of the tarp, which formed a sort of big, dusty cave.

A tire like a truck's loomed up a little way away in the gloom, but it was far more knobby than any she had seen.

"Oh. It's just a truck," she said, uncertainly. "You've got a truck in here, have you?"

"No," said Dorcas. "It's a Cat."

Grimma's response was impressive. She spun around in an effort to see in every direction at once.

"Where? Where?" she screamed. "You idiot! You brought us where there's a *cat*?"

Dorcas said nothing. He just pointed upward.

Grimma looked up. And then looked up some more. Into the mouth of the Cat.

Thirteen

IV.   Dorcas said, This is the Cat, Great Beast
with teeth.

V.   Needs Must. If we are driven, let us
Drive.

        —From the *Book of Nome, Cat II, v. IV–V*

Sometimes words need music too. Sometimes the descriptions are not enough. Books should be written with soundtracks, like films.

Something deep, on an organ, perhaps.

Grimma stared. Soundtrack *on:*

Deedle-dah-DEEdleDAHda-dum

It can't really be alive, she thought desperately. It's not really about to bite me. Dorcas wouldn't have brought me in here if he knew there was a monster about to bite me. I'm not going to be frightened. I'm not frightened at all. I am a thinking nome and I'm not *frightened*!

"I think the knobby wheels are just to make it grip the ground better," said Dorcas, his voice sounding a long way off. "Now, I've had a good look around it and, you know, there's nothing really wrong with it, it's just very old—"

Grimma's gaze travelled along the huge yellow neck.

Deedle-dah—deedle-dah-DUM

"Then I thought, I'm sure it could be started up. These diesel engines are quite easy really, and of course there were pictures in one of the books, although I'm not sure about these pipes, hydraulics I think its called, but there was this book on one of the benches, *Workshop Manual,* and I've put grease on things and cleaned it up," Dorcas gabbled.

Dah-dah-dah-DUM

"I suppose the humans, or whatever, knew they would be coming back, and I've been up and looked at the controls and, you know, it's probably easier than the truck was, only of course there's these extra levers for the hydraulics, but that shouldn't be a problem if there's enough gas, which . . ."

He stopped, aware of her silence.

"Is there something the matter?" he said.

"What *is* it?" said Grimma.

"I was just telling you," said Dorcas. "It's fascinating. You see, these pipes pump some sort of stuff which made those parts up there move, and those pistons are forced out, which makes the arm thing over there—"

"I didn't ask you what it does, I asked you what it *is,*" said Grimma, impatiently. "Because I know one thing. It's not a cat, Dorcas."

"You're wrong about that," said Dorcas. "See what's painted on it. Just up there, look."

She looked where he pointed. Grimma's brow wrinkled.

"C . . . A . . . T," she said. "Cat? But . . . but . . . Dorcas, that *can't* be right. Not really right. Look, a cat's got, well, whiskers. And hair. And it's a *whole* lot smaller."

"Dunno," said Dorcas, and he shrugged. "It's written right there. I'm not about to argue with things that are written right there. Maybe it's a *big* cat. Maybe all the whiskers dropped out a long time ago. You know? Like some old nomes lose their hair?"

"W-well," said Grimma, uncertainly. "But even the shape isn't right, and—"

"What do I know about this?" said Dorcas. "I'm not an expert in natural history. Anyway, come over to this side."

She followed him dreamily, and, once more, stared into the darkness under the tarp.

"There," he said. "There's no mistaking what *they* are, I hope."

"Oh, my," said Grimma, and raised her hand to her mouth.

"Yes," said Dorcas. "That's what I thought. When I first found this I thought, oh, it's a sort of truck, well, well, and then I walked up here and I found that it was a truck with—"

"Teeth," said Grimma, softly. "Great big metal teeth. A mouth at both ends?"

"That's right," said Dorcas proudly. "The Cat. A sort of truck. A truck with two heads. A truck with teeth."

Dah-DUM

"Does it—does it work?" said Grimma.

"It should. It should. I've tested what I can. Basic principle *is* like a truck, but there's a lot of extra levers and things—"

"Why didn't you tell me about this before?" Grimma demanded.

"Dunno. Because I didn't have to, I suppose," said Dorcas.

"But it's *huge*. You can't keep something like this to yourself!"

"Everyone has to have something they can keep to themselves," said Dorcas vaguely. "Anyway, the size isn't important. It's just so, well, so perfect." Dorcas patted a knobby tire. "You know, you said humans think someone made the world in a week? When I saw the Cat for the first time I thought, okay, this is what he used."

He stared up into the shadows.

"First thing we've got to do is get the tarp off," he said. "It'll be very heavy, so we'll need lots of people. You'd better warn them. The Cat can be a bit scary when you see it for the first time."

"Didn't frighten me a bit," said Grimma.

"I know," said Dorcas. "I was watching your face."

* * *

The nomes looked expectantly at Grimma.

"The thing to remember," she said, "is that it's just a machine. Just a sort of truck. But when you first see it, it can be rather frightening, so hold on to small children's hands. And run smartly backward when the tarp comes down."

There was a chorus of nods.

"All right. Grab hold."

Six hundred nomes spat on their hands and grasped the edge of the heavy cloth.

"When I say pull, I want you to pull."

The nomes took the strain.

"*Pull!*"

The creases in the tarp flattened out and disappeared.

"*Pull!*"

It began to move. Then, as it slid over the Cat's angular shape, its own weight started to tug at it.

"*Run!*"

It came down like an oily green avalanche, piling up into a mountain of folds, but no one bothered about it because the sun shone through the dusty, cobwebbed windows and made the Cat glow.

Several nomes screamed. Mothers picked up their children. There was a movement toward the doors.

The light twinkled on the tips of the teeth.

It *does* look like a head, Grimma thought. On a long neck. And he's got another one at the other end. What am I saying? *It* has got another one at the other end.

"I said it's all right!" she shouted over the rising din. "Look! It's not even moving!"

"Hey!" shouted another voice. She looked up. Nooty and Sacco had climbed out along the Cat's neck, and were sitting there, waving cheerfully.

That did it. The tide of nomes reached the wall and stopped. You always feel foolish, running away from something that isn't chasing you. They hesitated and then slowly inched their way back.

"Well, well," said Granny Morkie, hobbling forward. "So that's what they look like. I always wondered."

Grimma stared at her.

"What what look like?" she said.

"Oh, the big diggers," said Granny. "They'd all gone when I was born, but our dad saw 'em. Great big yellow things with teeth that et dirt, he said. I always thought he was having me on."

The Cat was still not eating people. Some of the more adventurous nomes started to climb on it.

"It was when the big highway was built," Granny went on, leaning on her stick. "They were all over the place, Dad said. Big yellow things with teeth and knobby tires."

Grimma stared at her with the kind of expression reserved for people who turn out, against all expectation, to have interesting and secret histories.

"And there was others too," the old woman went on. "Things that shoved dirt in piles and everything. This would have been, oh, fifteen years ago now. Never thought I'd see one."

"You mean the highways were *made*?" said Grimma. The Cat was covered with young nomes now. She could see Dorcas in the back of the cab, explaining what various levers did.

"That's what he said," said Granny. "You didn't think they was natch'ral, did you?"

"Oh. No. No. Of course not," said Grimma. "Don't be silly."

And she thought, I wonder if Dorcas is right? Perhaps everything was made. Everything in the whole world. Some parts early, some parts later. You start with hills and clouds and things, and then you add highways and Stores. Perhaps the job of humans is to make the world, and they're still doing it. That's why the machines have to suit them.

Gurder would have understood this sort of thing. I wish he were back.

And then Masklin would be back too.

She tried to think about something else.

Knobby tires. That was a good start. The Cat's back wheels were nearly as high as a human. It doesn't need highways. Of course it doesn't. It *makes* highways. So it has to be able to go where highways aren't.

She pushed her way through the crowds to the back of the cab, where another group of nomes were already nomehandling a plank into position, and scrambled up to where Dorcas was trying to make himself heard in the middle of an excited crowd.

"You're going to drive this out of here?" she demanded.

He looked up.

"Oh, yes," he said happily. "I think so. I hope so. I imagine we've got at least an hour before any more humans come, and it's not a lot different from a truck."

"We know how to do it!" shouted one of the younger nomes. "My dad told me all about the strings and stuff!"

Grimma looked around the cab. It seemed to be full of levers.

It'd been more than half a year since the Long Drive, and she'd never taken much notice of mechanical things, but she couldn't help thinking the old truck cab had been a lot less crowded. There had been some pedals and a lever and the steering wheel, and that had been about it.

She turned back to Dorcas.

"Are you sure?" she asked.

"No," he said. "You know I'm never sure. But a lot of the controls are for its mou—for the bucket. The thing with the teeth in it. At the end of its neck. I mean, the control arms. We needn't bother with them. They're amazingly ingenious, though, and all you have to do—"

"Where's everyone going to sit? There isn't much room."

Dorcas shrugged. "I suppose the older people

can travel in the cab. The youngsters will have to hang on where they can. We can wrap wires and things around the place. For handholds, I mean. Look, don't worry. We'll be driving in the light and we don't have to go fast."

"And then we'll get to the barn, won't we, Dorcas?" said Nooty. "Where it'll be warm and there's lots of food."

"I hope so," said Dorcas. "Now, let's get on with things. We haven't got much time. Where's Sacco with the battery?"

Grimma thought, Will there be lots of food at the barn? Where did we get that idea? Angalo said that turnips or something were stored up there, and there may be some potatoes. That's not exactly a feast.

Her stomach, thinking thoughts of its own, rumbled in disagreement. It had been a very long night to pass on a tiny piece of cheese sandwich.

Anyway, we can't stay here now. Anywhere will be better than here.

"Dorcas," she said, "Is there anything I can help with?"

He looked up. "You could read the instruction book," he said. "See if it says how to drive it."

"Don't you know?"

"Er. Not in so many words. Not *exactly*. I mean, I know how to do it, it's just that I don't know what to do."

It was under the bench on one side of the shed. Grimma propped it up and tried to concentrate despite the noise. I bet he does know, she thought. But this is his moment, and he doesn't want me getting in the way.

The nomes moved like people with a purpose. Things were far too bad to spend time grumbling. Funny thing, she thought as she turned the dirty pages, that people only seem to stop complaining when things get really bad. That's when they start using words like pulling together, shoulders to the wheel, and noses to the grindstone. She'd found "nose to the grindstone" in a book. Apparently it meant "to keep on with things." She didn't see why people were supposed to work hard if you ground their noses; it seemed more likely that they'd work hard if you promised to grind their noses if they didn't.

It had been the same with "Road Works Ahead" on the Long Drive. The road ahead works. How could it mean anything else? But the road had been full of holes. Where was the sense in that? Words ought to mean what they meant.

She turned the page.

There was a big brown ring on this one, where a human had put down a cup.

And the words Caterpillar Tractor Company. She gave them a blank look.

This is just what I mean, she thought. A caterpillar is a baby butterfly. A tractor is a sort of truck humans use in fields. Company is what you have when you're not alone. The words all mean something, and then they get put together, and who knows what they mean then?

Across the floor a group of nomes swarmed around the slowly moving bulk of the battery. They were rolling it on rusty ball bearings.

The can of fuel wobbled after it.

Grimma turned another page and stared at the pictures of levers with numbers on them. Suddenly people were keen on the barn, she thought. Suddenly, when things were not just averagely awful but promising to be really dreadful, they seemed almost happy. Masklin had known about that. It's amazing what people would do, he said, if you found the right place to push.

She went on reading.

Back hoe. Now, what was that supposed to mean? Maybe you had to shout instructions to the Cat? Like, maybe, "Back, hoe!" And "Forward, hey!" Or maybe not?

She stared at the pages, and tried to get interested in levers.

The clouds running before the sun were spreading across the pink of the sky. Red sky in the morning, Grimma had read once. It meant sailors were unhappy. She didn't know what sailors were, though, or why they made the sky red when they were unhappy.

In the dark office the human awoke, mooed for a while, and tried to jerk free of the cobweb of wires that held it down. After a lot of effort it wriggled most of one arm free.

What the human did next would have surprised most nomes. It caught hold of a chair and, with a great deal of grunting, managed to tip it over. It pulled it across the floor, manipulated the leg under a couple of strands of wire, and heaved.

A minute later it was sitting upright, pulling more wires free.

Its huge eyes fell on the scrap of paper on the floor.

It stared at it for a moment, rubbing its arms, and then it picked up the telephone.

Dorcas prodded vaguely at a wire.

"Are you sure the battery is connected the right way, sir?" said Sacco.

"I can tell the difference between red wires and black wires, you know," said Dorcas mildly, prodding another wire.

"Then perhaps the battery doesn't have enough electricity," said Grimma helpfully, trying to see over their shoulders. "Perhaps it's all run to the bottom, or gone dry."

Dorcas and Sacco exchanged glances.

"Electricity doesn't sink," said Dorcas patiently. "Or dry up, as far as I know. It's either there or it isn't. Excuse me." He peered up into the mass of wires again, and gave one a poke. There was a pop, and a fat blue spark.

"It's there all right," he added. "It's just that it isn't where it should be."

Grimma walked back across the greasy floor of the cab. Groups of nomes were standing around, waiting. Hundreds of them were clutching the wires attached to the big steering wheel above them. Other teams stood by with bits of wood pressing, like battering rams, on the pedals.

"Just a bit of a delay," she said. "All the electricity's got lost."

There were nomes everywhere. On the Long Drive there had been a whole truck for them. But the Cat's cab was smaller, and people had to pack themselves in where they could.

What a ragged bunch, Grimma thought. And it was true. Even in the sudden rush from the Store the nomes had been able to bring a lot of stuff. And they had been plump and well dressed.

Now they were thinner and leaner and much dirtier and all they were taking with them were the torn and grubby clothes they stood up in. Even the books had been left behind. A hundred books took up the space of three hundred nomes, and while Grimma privately thought that some of the books were more useful than many of the nomes, she'd accepted Dorcas's promise that they would come back one day and try to retrieve them from their hiding place under the floor.

Well, thought Grimma. We tried. We really made an effort. We came to the quarry to dig in, look after ourselves, live proper lives. And we failed. We thought all we had to do was bring the right things from the Store, but we brought a lot of wrong things too. Next time we'll need to go as far away from humans as possible, and I don't actually think anywhere is far enough.

She climbed up onto the rickety driving platform, which had been made by tying a plank across the cab. There were even nomes on this. They watched her expectantly.

At least driving the Cat should be easier. The leaders of the teams on the controls could see her, so she wouldn't have to mess around with semaphore and pieces of thread as they'd done when they left the Store. And a lot of the nomes had done this before too . . .

She heard Dorcas shout, "Try it this time!"

There was a *click*. There was a *whirr*. Then the Cat roared.

The sound bounced around the cave of the shed. It was so loud and so deep it wasn't really sound at all, just something that turned the air hard and then hit you with it. Nomes flung themselves flat on the trembling deck of the cab.

Grimma, clutching at her ears, saw Dorcas running across the floor, waving his hands. The team on the accelerator pedal gave him a "Who, us?" look and stopped pushing.

The sound died down to a deep, rumbling purr, a *mummummummum* that still had a feel-it-in-the-bone quality. Dorcas hurried back and climbed, with a lot of stopping for breath, up to the plank.

When he got there he sat down and rubbed his brow.

"I'm getting too old for this sort of thing," he said. "When a nome gets to a certain age, it's time to stop stealing giant vehicles. Well-known fact. Anyway. It's ticking over nicely. You might as well take us out."

"What, all by myself?" said Grimma.

"Yes. Why not?"

"It's just that, well, I thought Sacco or someone would be up here." I thought a male nome would be driving, she thought.

"They'd *like* to," said Dorcas. "They'd *love* to. And we'd be zipping all over the place, I don't doubt it, with them crying 'yippee!' and whatnot. No. I want a nice peaceful drive across the fields, thank you very much. The gentle touch."

He leaned down.

"Everyone ready down there?" he yelled.

There was a chorus of nervous "yesses," and one or two cheerful ones.

"I wonder if putting Sacco in charge of the go-faster pedal is really a good idea," mused Dorcas. He straightened up.

"Er. You're not *worried*, are you?" he said.

Grimma snorted. "What? Me? No. Of course not. It does not," she added, "present a problem."

"*O-kay,*" he said. "Let's go."

There was silence, except for the deep thrumming of the engine.

Grimma paused.

If Masklin were here, she thought, he'd do this better than me. No one mentions him anymore. Or Angalo. Or Gurder. They don't like thinking about them. That must be something nomes learned hundreds of years ago, in this world full of foxes and rushing things and a hundred nasty ways to die. If someone is missing, you must stop thinking about them, you must put them out of your mind. But I think about him all the time.

I just went on about the frogs in the flowers, and I never thought about his dreams.

Dorcas gently put his arm around her. She was shaking. *Everyone* was shaking to the deep chugging of the motor. But she was shaking worse.

"We should have sent some people to the airport to see what happened to him," she muttered. "It would have showed that we cared, and—"

"We didn't have the time, and we didn't have the people," said Dorcas softly. "When he comes back we can explain about that. He's bound to understand."

"Yes," she whispered.

"And now," said Dorcas, standing back, "let's go!"

Grimma took a deep breath.

"First gear," she bellowed, "and go forward verrrry slowly."

The teams pushed and pulled their way over the deck. There was a slight shudder and the engine noise dropped. The Cat lurched forward and jolted to a stop. The motor coughed and died.

Dorcas looked thoughtfully at his fingernails.

"Hand brake, hand brake, hand brake," he hummed softly.

Grimma glared at him, and cupped her hands around her mouth. "Take the hand brake off!" she shouted. "Right! *Now*, get into first gear and go forward very slowly!"

There was a *click*, and silence.

"Startthemotor, startthemotor, startthemotor," murmured Dorcas, rocking back and forth on his heels.

Grimma sagged. "Put everything back where it was and start the motor," she screamed.

Nooty, in charge of the hand brake team, called up, "Do you want the hand brake on or off, miss?"

"What?"

"You haven't told us what to do with the hand brake, miss," said Sacco. The nomes with him started to grin.

Grimma shook a finger at him. "Listen, mister," she snapped, "if I have to come down there and tell you what to do with the hand brake, you'll all be *extremely sorry*, all right? Now stop giggling like that and *get this thing moving! Quickly!*"

There was a click. The Cat howled again and started to move. A cheer went up from the nomes.

"Right," said Grimma. "That's more like it."

"The doors, the doors, the doors, we didn't open the doors," hummed Dorcas.

"Of course we didn't open the doors," said Grimma as the digger began to go faster. "We *never* open the doors! What do we need to open the doors for? This is the Cat!"

Fourteen

V.   There is nothing that can *be* in our way,
       for this is the Cat, that laughs at barriers,
       and purrs *brrm-brrm*.
            —From the *Book of Nome, Cat III, v. V*

It was an old shed. It was a very rusty shed. It was
a shed that wobbled in high winds. The only thing
even vaguely new about it was the padlock on the
door, which the Cat hit at about six miles an hour.
The rickety building rang like a gong, leapt off its
foundations, and was dragged halfway across the
quarry before it fell apart in a shower of rust and
smoke. The Cat emerged like a very angry chick
from a very old egg and then rolled to a stop.

Grimma picked herself up from the plank and
nervously started to pick bits of rust off herself.

"We've stopped," she said vaguely, her ears still
ringing. "Why have we stopped, Dorcas?"

He didn't bother to try to get up. The thump of
the Cat hitting the door had knocked all the breath
out of him.

"I think," he said, "that everyone might have been flung about a little. Why did you want it to go so fast?"

"Sorry!" Sacco called up. "Bit of a misunderstanding there, I think!"

Grimma pulled herself together. "Well," she said, "I got us out, anyway. I've got the hang of it now. We'll just . . . we'll just . . . we'll . . ."

Dorcas heard her voice fade into silence. He looked up.

There was a truck parked in front of the quarry. And three humans were running toward the Cat in big, floating bounds.

"Oh, dear," he said.

"Didn't it read my note?" asked Grimma.

"I'm afraid it did," said Dorcas. "Now, we shouldn't panic. We've got a choice. We can either—"

"Go forward," snapped Grimma. "Right now!"

"No, no," said Dorcas weakly, "I wasn't going to suggest that—"

"First gear!" Grimma commanded. "And lots of fast!"

"No, you don't want to do that," Dorcas murmured.

"Watch me," said Grimma. "I *warned* them! They *can* read, we know they can read! If they're really intelligent, they're intelligent enough to know better!"

The Cat gathered speed.

"You mustn't do this," said Dorcas. "We've always kept away from humans!"

"They don't keep away from us!" shouted Grimma.

"But—"

"They demolished the Store, they tried to stop us from escaping, now they're taking our quarry, *and they don't even know what we are!*" said Grimma. "Remember the gardening department in the Store? Those horrible garden ornament statues? Well, I'm going to show them *real* nomes . . ."

"You can't beat humans!" shouted Dorcas above the roar of the engine. "They're too big! You're too small!"

"They may be big," said Grimma, "and I may be small. But *I'm* the one with the great big truck. With *teeth.*" She leaned over the plank. "Everyone hang on down there," she shouted. "This may be rough."

It had dawned on the great slow creatures outside that something was wrong. They stopped their lumbering charge and, very slowly, tried to dodge out of the way. Two of them managed to leap into the empty office as the Cat bowled past.

"I see," said Grimma. "They must think we're stupid. Take a big left turn. More. More. Now stop. Okay." She rubbed her hands together.

"What are you going to do?" whispered Dorcas, terrified.

Grimma leaned over the plank.

"Sacco," she said. "You see those other levers?"

* * *

The pale round blobs of the humans' faces appeared at the dusty windows of the shed.

The Cat was twenty feet away, vibrating gently in the early morning mist. Then the engine roared. The big front shovel came up, catching the sunlight.

The Cat sprang forward, bouncing across the quarry floor and taking out one wall of the shed like ripping the lid off a can. The other walls and the roof folded up gently, as if it were a house of cards with the ace of spades flipped away.

The digger careened around in a big circle, so that when the two humans crawled out of the wreckage it was the first thing they saw. Throbbing, with the big metal mouth poised to bite.

They ran.

They ran almost as fast as nomes.

"I've always wanted to do that," said Grimma, in a satisfied voice. "Now, where did the other human go?"

"Back to the truck, I think," said Dorcas weakly.

"Fine," said Grimma. "Now—lots of right, Sacco. Stop. Now forward, slowly."

"Can we sort of stop this and just go now? Please?" pleaded Dorcas.

"The humans' truck is in the way," said Grimma, reasonably enough. "They've stopped right in the entrance."

"Then we're trapped," said Dorcas.

Grimma laughed. It wasn't a very amusing sound. Dorcas suddenly felt almost as sorry for the humans as he was feeling for himself.

The humans must have been having similar thoughts, if humans had thoughts. He could see their pale faces watching the Cat lurch toward them.

They're wondering why they can't see a human inside, he thought. They can't work it out. Here's this machine, moving all by itself. It's a puzzler, for humans.

They reached some sort of conclusion, though. He saw both truck doors fly open and the humans jump out just as the Cat . . .

There was a crunch, and the truck jerked as the Cat hit it. The knobby wheels spun for a moment, and then the truck rolled backward. Clouds of steam poured out.

"That's for Nisodemus," said Grimma.

"I thought you didn't like him," said Dorcas.

"Yes, but he was a nome."

Dorcas nodded. They were all, when you got right down to it, nomes. It was just as well to remember whose side you were on.

"May I suggest you change gear?" he said quietly.

"Why? What's wrong with the one we've got?"

"You'll be able to push better if you go down a gear. Trust me."

* * *

Humans were watching. They *were* watching, because a machine rolling around by itself is something that you do watch, even if you've just had to climb a tree or hide behind a hedge.

They saw the Cat roll backward, change gear with a roar, and attack the truck again. The windows shattered.

Dorcas was really unhappy about this.

"You're killing a truck," he said.

"Don't be silly," said Grimma. "It's a machine. Just bits of metal. Back, hoe!"

"Yes, but someone made it," said Dorcas. "They must be very hard to make. I hate destroying things that are hard to make."

"They ran over Nisodemus," said Grimma. "And when we used to live in a hole, nomes were always being squashed by cars. Forward, hey!"

"Yes, but nomes aren't hard to make," said Dorcas, hanging on grimly as they smashed into the truck again. "You just need other nomes."

"Back, hoe! You're weird. Forward, hey!"

The Cat struck again. One of the truck's headlights exploded. Dorcas winced.

Then the truck was pushed clear. Smoke was billowing out from it now, where fuel had spilled over the hot engine. The Cat backed off and rumbled around it. The nomes were really getting the hang of him now.

"Right," said Grimma. "Straight ahead." She

nudged Dorcas. "We'll go and find this barn now, shall we?"

"Just go down the road, and I think there's a gateway into the fields," Dorcas mumbled. "It had an actual gate in it," he added. "I suppose it would be too much to ask you to let us open it first?"

Behind them the truck burst into flames. Not spectacularly, but in a workmanlike way, as if it were going to go on burning all day. Dorcas saw a human take off its coat and flap uselessly at the fire. He felt quite sorry for it.

The Cat rolled unopposed down the dirt road. Some of the nomes started to sing as they sweated over the ropes.

"Now, then," said Grimma, "where's this gateway? Through the gate and across the fields, you said, and—"

"It's just before you get to the car with the flashing lights on top," said Dorcas slowly. "The one that's just coming up the road."

They stared at it.

"Cars with lights on the top are bad news," said Grimma.

"You're right there," said Dorcas. "They're often full of humans who very seriously want to know what's going on. There were lots of them down at the railroad."

Grimma looked along the hedge.

"This is the gateway coming up, is it?" she said. "Yes."

Grimma leaned down.

"Slow down and turn sharp right," she said.

The teams swung into action. Sacco even changed gear without being asked. Nomes hung like spiders from the steering wheel, hauling it around.

There *was* a gate in the gateway. But it was old and held to the post with bits of string in proper agricultural fashion. It wouldn't have stopped anything very determined, and it had no chance with the Cat.

Dorcas winced again.

The field on the other side was brown soil. Corrugated earth, the nomes called it, after the corrugated cardboard you sometimes got in the packing department in the Store. There was snow between the furrows. The big wheels churned it into mud.

Dorcas was half expecting the car to follow them. It stopped instead, and two humans in dark blue suits got out and started to lumber across the field. There's no stopping humans, he thought glumly. They're like the weather.

The field ran gently uphill, around the quarry. The Cat's engine thudded.

There was a fence ahead, with a grassy field beyond it. The wire parted with a twang. Dorcas watched it roll back, and wondered whether Grimma would let him stop and collect a bit of it. You always knew where you were with wire.

The humans were still following. Out of the corner of his eye, because up here there was altogether too much Outside to look at, Dorcas saw flashing lights on the highway, far away.

He pointed them out to Grimma.

"I know," she said. "I've seen them. But what else could we have done?" she added desperately. "Gone off and lived in the flowers like good little *pixies?*"

"I don't know," said Dorcas wearily. "I'm not sure about anything anymore."

Another wire fence twanged. There was shorter grass up here, and the ground curved.

And then there was nothing but sky, and the Cat speeding up as the wheels bounced over the field at the top of the hill.

Dorcas had never seen so much sky. There was nothing around them, just a bit of scrub in the distance. And it was silent. Well, not silent at all, because of the Cat's roar. But it looked like the kind of place that *would* be silent if diggers full of desperate nomes weren't thundering across it.

Some sheep ran out of the way.

"There's the barn up ahead, that stone building on the horiz—" Grimma began. Then she said, "Are you all right, Dorcas?"

"If I keep my eyes shut," he whispered.

"You look dreadful."

"I *feel* worse."

"But you've been Outside before."

"Grimma, we're the highest thing there is! There's nothing higher than us for miles, or whatever you call those things! If I open my eyes I'll fall into the sky!"

Grimma leaned down to the perspiring drivers.

"Right just a bit!" she shouted. "That's it! Now, all the fast you can!"

"Hold on to the Cat!" she shouted, as the engine noise grew. "You know *he* can't fly!"

The machine bumped up on a stony track that led in the general direction of the distant barn. Dorcas risked opening one eye.

He'd never been to the barn. Was anyone certain there was food there, or was it just a guess? Perhaps at least it'd be warm.

But there was a flashing light near it, coming toward them.

"Why won't they leave us *alone?*" shouted Grimma. "Stop!"

The Cat rolled to a halt. The engine ticked over in the chilly air.

"This must lead down to another highway," said Dorcas.

"We can't go back," said Grimma.

"No."

"Or forward."

"No."

Grimma drummed her fingers on the Cat's metal.

"Have you got any other ideas?"

"We could try going across the fields," said Dorcas.

"Where would that take us?" said Grimma.

"Away from here, for a start."

"But we wouldn't know where we were going!" said Grimma.

Dorcas shrugged. "It's either that or paint flowers."

Grimma tried to smile.

"And those little wings wouldn't suit me," she said.

"What's going on up there?" Sacco yelled up.

"We ought to tell people," Grimma whispered. "Everyone thinks we're going to the barn."

She looked around. The car was closer, bumping heavily over the rough track. The two humans were still coming the other way. "Don't humans ever give up?" she said to herself.

She leaned over the edge of the plank.

"Some left, Sacco," she said. "And then just go steadily."

The Cat bounced off the track and rolled over the cold grass. There was another wire fence in the far distance, and a few more sheep.

We don't know where we're going, she thought. The only important thing is to *go*. Masklin knew it. This isn't our world.

"Perhaps we should have talked to humans," she said aloud.

"No, you were right," said Dorcas. "In this world everything belongs to humans and we would belong to them too. There wouldn't be any room for us to be *us*."

The fence came closer. There was a road on the

other side. Not a dirt road, but a proper road with black gravel on it.

"Right or left?" said Grimma. "What do you think?"

"It doesn't matter," said Dorcas as the digger twanged through the fence.

"We'll try going left, then," she said. "Slow down, Sacco! Left a bit. More. More. Steady at that. Oh, no!"

There was another car in the distance. It had flashing lights on the top.

Dorcas risked a look behind them.

There was another flashing light there.

"No," he said.

"What?" said Grimma.

"Just a little while ago you asked if humans ever gave up," he said. "They don't."

"Stop," said Grimma.

The teams trotted obediently across the Cat's floor. The digger rolled gently to a halt again, engine ticking over.

"This is it," said Dorcas.

"Are we at the barn yet?" a nome called up.

"No," said Grimma. "Not yet. Nearly."

Dorcas made a face.

"We might as well accept it now," he said. "You'll end up waving a stick with a star on it. I just hope they don't force me to mend their shoes."

Grimma looked thoughtful. "If we drove as hard as we could at that car coming toward us—" she began.

"No," said Dorcas, firmly. "It really wouldn't solve anything."

"It'd make me feel a lot better," said Grimma.

She looked around at the fields.

"Why's it gone all dark?" she said. "We can't have been running all day. It was early morning when we started out."

"Doesn't time fly when you're enjoying yourself?" said Dorcas gloomily. "And I don't like milk much. I don't mind doing their housework if I *don't* have to drink milk, but—"

"Just *look*, will you?"

Darkness was spreading across the fields.

"It might be an ellipse," said Dorcas. "I read about them. It all goes dark when the Sun covers the Moon. And possibly vice versa," he added doubtfully.

The car ahead of them squealed to a halt, crashed backward across the road into a stone wall, and came to an abrupt stop.

In the field by the road the sheep were running away. It wasn't the ordinary panic of sheep ordinarily disturbed. They had their heads down and were pounding across the ground with one aim in mind. They were sheep who had decided that this was no time to waste energy panicking when it could be used for galloping away as fast as possible.

A loud and unpleasant humming noise filled the air.

"My word," Dorcas said weakly. "They're pretty darn terrifying, these ellipses." Down below, the nomes *were* panicking. They weren't sheep, they could all think for themselves, and when you started to think hard about sudden darkness and mysterious humming noises, panicking seemed a logical idea.

Little lines of crawling blue fire crackled over the Cat's battered paintwork. Dorcas felt his hair standing on end.

Grimma stared upward.

The sky was totally black.

"It's . . . all . . . right," she said slowly. "Do you know, I think it's all right!"

Dorcas looked at his hands. Sparks crackled off his fingertips.

"It is, is it?" was all he could think of.

"That isn't night, it's a shadow. There's something huge floating above us."

"And that's better than night, is it?" said Dorcas.

"I think so. Come on, let's get off."

She shinned down the rope to the Cat's deck. She was smiling madly. That was almost as terrifying as everything else put together. They weren't used to Grimma smiling.

"Give me a hand," she said. "We've got to get down. So he can be sure it's us."

They looked at her in astonishment as she wrestled with the gangplank.

"Come *on,*" she repeated. "Help me, can't you?"

"He? Who he?" said Dorcas. "What he? What do you mean?"

"Him," said Grimma. "I know it's him. You people—help me!"

They helped. Sometimes, when you're totally confused, you'll listen to anyone who seems to have any sort of aim in mind. They grabbed the plank and shoved it out of the back of the cab until it tilted and swung down toward the road.

At least there wasn't so much sky now. The blue was a thin line around the edge of the solid darkness overhead.

Not entirely solid. When Dorcas's eyes grew used to it, he could make out squares and rectangles and circles.

Nomes scurried down the plank and milled around on the road below, uncertain whether to run or stay.

Above them one of the dark squares in the shadow moved aside. There was a clank, and then a rectangle of darkness whirred down very gently, like an elevator without wires, and landed softly on the road. It was quite big.

There was something on it. Something in a pot. Something red and yellow and green.

The nomes craned forward to see what it was.

Fifteen

I.   Thus ended the journey of the Cat, and
     the nomes fled, looking not behind.
     —From the *Book of Nome, Stranger Frogs I, v. I*

Dorcas clambered down awkwardly onto the Cat's
oily deck. It was empty now, except for the bits of
string and wood that the nomes had used.

They've dropped things just any old way, he
thought, listening to the distant chattering of the
nomes. It's not right, leaving litter. Poor old Cat
deserves more than this.

There was some sort of excitement going on outside, but he didn't pay it much attention.

He bumbled around for a bit, trying to coil up
the string and push the wood into neat piles. He
pulled down the wires that had let the Cat taste the
electricity. He got down on his hands and knees
and tried to rub out the muddy footprints.

The Cat made noises, even with the engine
stopped. Little pops and sizzles, and the occasional
ping.

It was going to sleep again. Sleeping was something cats did a lot of, he'd heard.

Dorcas sat down and leaned against the yellow metal. He didn't know what was going on. It was so far outside anything he'd ever seen before that his mind wasn't letting him worry about it.

Perhaps that thing up there is just another machine, he thought wearily. A machine for making night come down suddenly.

He reached out and stroked the Cat.

"Well done," he said.

Sacco and Nooty found him sitting with his head against the cab wall, staring vacantly at his feet.

"Everyone's been looking for you!" Sacco said. "It's like an airplane without wings! It's just floating there in the air! So you must come and tell us what makes it go . . . I say, are you all right?"

"Hmm?"

"Are you all right?" said Nooty. "You look rather odd."

Dorcas nodded slowly. "Just a bit worn out," he said.

"Yes, but, you see, we need you," said Sacco insistently.

Dorcas groaned and allowed himself to be helped to his feet. He took a last look around the cab.

"He really went, didn't he?" he said. "He really went very well. All things considered. For his age."

He tried to give Sacco a cheerful look.

"What are you talking about?" said Sacco.

"All that time in that shed. Since the world was

made, perhaps. And I just greased him and fuelled him up and away he went," said Dorcas.

"The machine? Oh, yes. Well done," said Sacco.

"But—" Nooty pointed upward.

Dorcas shrugged.

"Oh, I'm not bothered about that," he said. "It's probably Masklin's doing. Perfectly simple explanation. Grimma is right. It's probably that flying thing he went off to get."

"But something has come out of it!" said Nooty.

"Not Masklin, you mean?"

"It's some kind of plant!"

Dorcas sighed. Always one thing after another. He patted the Cat again.

"Well, *I* care," he said.

He straightened up, and turned to the others.

"All right," he said. "Show me."

It was in a metal pot in the middle of the floating platform. The nomes craned and tried to climb on one another's shoulders to look at it, and none of them knew what it was except for Grimma, who was staring at it with a strange quiet smile on her face.

It was a branch from a tree. On the branch was a flower the size of a bucket.

If you climbed high enough, you could see that, held within its glistening petals, was a pool of water. And from the depths of the pool little yellow frogs stared up at the nomes.

"Have *you* any idea what it is?" said Sacco.

Dorcas smiled. "Masklin's found out that it's a good idea to send a girl flowers," he said. "And I think everything's all right." He glanced at Grimma.

"Yes, but *what* is it?"

"I seem to remember it's called a bromeliad," said Dorcas. "It grows on the top of very tall trees in wet forests a long way away, and little frogs spend their whole lives in it. Your whole life in one flower. Imagine that. Grimma once said she thought it was the most astonishing thing in the world."

Sacco bit his lip thoughtfully.

"Well, there's electricity," he said. "Electricity is quite astonishing."

"Or hydraulics," said Nooty, taking his hand. "You told me hydraulics was fascinating."

"Masklin must have got it for her," said Dorcas, ignoring them. "Very literal-minded lad, that lad. Very active imagination."

He stared from the flower to the Cat, looking small and old under the humming shadow of the ship.

And felt, suddenly, quite cheerful. He was still tired enough to go to sleep standing up, but he felt his mind fizzing with ideas. Of course there were a lot of questions, but right now the answers didn't matter; it was enough just to enjoy the questions, and know that the world was full of astonishing things, and that he wasn't a frog.

Or at least he was the kind of frog who was interested in how flowers grew and whether you could get to other flowers if you jumped hard enough.

And just when you'd got out of the flower, and were feeling really proud of yourself, you'd look at the new, big, wide endless world around you.

And eventually you'd notice that it had petals around the horizon.

Dorcas grinned.

"I'd very much like to know," he said, "what Masklin has been doing these past few weeks."

About the Author

Terry Pratchett is the author of the highly acclaimed group of Discworld novels, which includes *The Color of Magic, The Light Fantastic,* and *Equal Rites.* Although these books were intended for adults, they have a devoted following among younger readers as well.

Diggers is Terry Pratchett's second book, following *Truckers,* in the Bromeliad trilogy for young adults about the adventures of the nomes. The adventures of Masklin, Gurder, and Angalo will be unfolded in the last Book of the Nomes.

Terry Pratchett lives with his family in England, where, he says, he grows carnivorous plants and tries to make computers do things they were never intended to do.